The woman was a "swallow"

She used her beauty and sex as a weapon, and Manning knew that if she was supposed to distract him that meant the real threat lurked somewhere else.

Suddenly, he saw it. A figure rose in the parking lot between a Buick and a station wagon, a large pistol held in a two-handed grip. The Phoenix Force pro instinctively ducked. The pistol hissed like a serpent, and something tugged at the corner of Manning's jacket as he bolted for the cover of a Chevy sedan. A second projectile sizzled and scraped the trunk lid of the sedan as Manning ducked behind the vehicle. That shot had come from a different direction, so there were at least two gunmen to deal with.

Manning realized something was stuck in his collar, and as he tugged on the jacket he stared down at the feathered end of a tranquilizer dart lodged in the sheepskin.

Manning shuffled to the front of the sedan, then stopped, trying to tune out the thumping of his pounding heart as he strained to detect any telltale sounds of his mysterious opponents. The Canadian heard soft patting sounds that could have been rubber soles against pavement. A slight electrical crackle may have been static from a two-way radio.

Don't jump to conclusions, he told himself. Jump the wrong way, you're dead.

Mack Bolan's

PHOENIX FORCE

PHOENIX FORCE

Tooth and Claw

Gar Wilson

A GOLD EAGLE BOOK FROM
WORLDWIDE

TORONTO · NEW YORK · LONDON · PARIS
AMSTERDAM · STOCKHOLM · HAMBURG
ATHENS · MILAN · TOKYO · SYDNEY

First edition November 1985

ISBN 0-373-61320-2

Special thanks and acknowledgment to
William Fieldhouse for his contributions to this work.

Printed in Canada

1

Lieutenant Colonel Vladimir Georgevich Burov marched into the plush office of the Committee for State Security—the Komitet Gosurdarstvennoy Bezopasnosti, better known as the KGB. The white-haired chairman sat behind his ornate brass-inlaid desk, clad in a black suit and tie and a white shirt with a collar as stiff as cardboard. This was the chairman's uniform. The coveted Order of Lenin was pinned to the left breast of his jacket.

A painting of Lenin hung on one wall and a color photograph of the most recent premier of the Soviet Union hung on another. The flag of the Union of Soviet Socialist Republics, the familiar red banner with yellow hammer and sickle, was mounted behind the chairman's desk. Across from it was another red flag bearing the emblem of a diamond-shaped shield bisected by a sword with a red star in the center, the symbol of the KGB.

The Soviet secret police has been an essential force in the USSR since the Russian revolution when it was known as the Cheka. It has been renamed many times since and has undergone numerous cosmetic changes purely for the sake of appearances. The same agency has been called the GPU, the NKVD, the NKGB and the MGB. Since 1954 it has been known as the KGB, but its function has always remained the same—to keep the Communist ruling elite in control of the USSR and to carry out the clandestine operations necessary for a "workers' revolution" throughout the world.

Thus, the old man seated behind the desk was one of the most powerful and feared men in the Soviet Union. Colo-

nel Burov was honored to be summoned to personally meet
with his supreme commander. Yet Burov felt fear and ap
prehension as he snapped his boot heels together and
smartly saluted.

"Lieutenant Colonel Burov, reporting as ordered, sir,"
the officer announced.

"Be seated, Colonel," the chairman replied, wearily re
turning the salute with a slight wave of his hand.

"*Spacibo*, Comrade Chairman." Burov thanked his boss
as he moved to one of four chairs in front of the desk.

The other three chairs were already occupied. Burov was
surprised to see that none of the men seated with him were
KGB. Two men wore Soviet army uniforms. On the shoulder boards of their uniforms, four red bars and a scarlet star
labeled the pair as majors. The younger of the army officers was more than six feet tall, very muscular and trim at
the waist. In his lap was a blue beret with a white parachute
badge capped by a red star. Burov recognized this as the
emblem of an airborne paratrooper.

The other army major appeared to be in his late forties,
about ten years older than the younger officer and perhaps
five years older than Burov. He was a bit paunchy at the
waist and his bloodshot eyes were surrounded by hooded
lids and fleshy bags. Burov outranked the older man, but he
noticed the major had been awarded both the Order of the
Red Flag and the Gold Star. Burov had been decorated with
the former honor, but the latter medal would never be
pinned on the KGB officer's chest.

The last man was the biggest surprise of the lot. He was
middle-aged, probably fity-six or fifty-seven. His dark gray
hair was combed back from a high forehead and his eyes
seemed weary yet very intelligent and constantly alert. The
most startling fact about the man was that he wasn't a Russian. He wore the uniform of a Bulgarian army officer with
the rank of full colonel on his shoulder boards. Most impressive of all were the military awards pinned to his tunic.
The Bulgarian wore the diamond-studded Marshal's Star
and the Gold Star of the Heroes of the People's Republic of

Bulgaria, the highest military honor awarded by that country. It was Bulgaria's equivalent of the Order of Victory in the USSR or the Medal of Honor in the United States.

"Perhaps I should introduce everyone," the KGB chairman began. "Lieutenant Colonel Burov is from the Second Main Directorate of the KGB. This, as I'm sure you all know, deals with foreign operations. Colonel Burov worked as a clandestine agent in certain English-speaking countries in the past. He is a very respected and honored operative. As you can see, he has been decorated for his contributions to helping our oppressed comrades of the world struggle against imperialism."

The chairman turned to the senior major. "Perhaps you've heard of Major Leonid Petrovich Potapov," the chairman began. "Major Potapov was awarded the Gold Star of Valor for rescuing a squad of Soviet soldiers who were nearly slaughtered by bandits in Afghanistan. Our peacekeeping troops were under attack by the local thugs, who are, of course, lackies of the American CIA. The Afghan trash had our brave fighting men pinned down with machine-gun fire until Major Potapov single-handedly killed every one of the bandit scum."

"I beg your pardon, Comrade Chairman," Potapov said with a shrug. "But there were only two Afghans...."

The chairman silenced him with a hard stare. "The major is a modest man. A true hero to the people of the Soviet Union and the cause of world socialism everywhere. What the rest of you may not know is that Major Potapov is a case officer for the Glavnoye Razvedyvatelnoye Upravleniye. It is indeed an honor that the KGB will be working with our sister organization from the General Staff."

The GRU, basically a military intelligence organization, was technically part of the Soviet army, although it frequently served the same functions as the KGB. The GRU was not as large or as powerful as the KGB, yet it was the second-to-largest intelligence network in the world, second only to the KGB itself. Occasionally the two organizations were forced into working together, a situation neither cared for.

"Major Aleksei Semyonovich Shalnev is, of course, an officer from our glorious parachute division," the chairman said as he introduced the young, muscular Russian. "He is a highly-trained commando who has served the interests of the Soviet Union and the struggle of the world revolution in campaigns in Africa, Poland and, most recently, Afghanistan. He is one of the finest fighting men in the world. A personification of the spirit of the Soviet people."

Major Shalnev's chest swelled with pride. Burov was familiar with the ego-stroking tactics used by the chairman. It was a form of propaganda. The Kremlin thrives on propaganda and it feeds propaganda to the public in tidal waves. Burov noticed that Major Potapov rolled his eyes toward the ceiling. Potapov clearly recognized the chairman's tactics as well, but he, unlike Burov, was foolish enough to express his opinion.

No wonder you're just a major, Potapov, Burov thought.

"Finally," the chairman continued, "our comrade from Bulgaria is Colonel Nikolai Ivanovich Kostov. The colonel is a great war hero who valiantly fought against the minions of Hitler's Nazis. Colonel Kostov served with the Red Lion resistance fighters in Greece, and after the war he was recruited into Bulgarian intelligence. He has served his country and the battle against imperialism ever since."

Every man in the room was aware of the fact that the People's Republic of Bulgaria is owned and operated by the Soviet Union. Of all the satellite countries of the iron curtain, none is more of total puppet than Bulgaria. Unlike Hungary, Czechoslovakia or East Germany, Bulgaria has never challenged the absolute authority of the Soviet Union.

The Bulgarian secret police is virtually an extension of the KGB. Kostov had been drafted into Department Eleven of the KGB's foreign service. Naturally, since Bulgarians are not Russians, they tended to get dirty assignments that the USSR didn't want to be directly connected with.

Every man in the room realized another fact. The Soviet Union has a premier, the general secretary of the party. However, the premier is a figurehead, appointed by the politburo to carry out the wishes of the politburo. The Soviet Union is actually run by the triumvirate, the three absolute powers of the party, the KGB and the army. Gathered together in the office of the KGB chairman were officers from two of the great Soviet powers. For this to happen, the politburo must also be involved.

Something had occurred that had obviously upset the inner circle of the Soviet government, and the men seated before the chairman wondered what earthshaking incident had disrupted the lords of Red Square. Perhaps the Soviet Union was planning a major invasion that required the skills of their top intelligence operatives, GRU as well as KGB.

"Gentlemen," the chairman began, "we are faced with an unusual problem...a rather embarrassing problem. During the past three and a half years no less than three and possibly as many as five major KGB operations of the Second Main Directorate have been ruined by an elite team of enemy commandos."

"A team of commandos, sir?" Major Potapov inquired. "A single team of men?"

"That is correct, Major," the chairman replied tensely. "And we believe this team consists of only five men."

The announcement stunned everyone present, except Colonel Kostov. The Bulgarian had already learned this information from firsthand experience

"Evidence concerning these commandos has been difficult to acquire," the chairman began. "We're not even certain how many incidents they were involved with. The first may have been a highly secret mission conducted within the United States itself. I can't give you all the details, but one of our moles was coordinating a group of Japanese zealots known as the Tigers of Justice. These Orientals were attempting to sabotage American nuclear power plants to encourage the warmongers of the United States to cease building bombs that were a threat to the existence of the entire world."

Major Potapov managed to keep a straight face. The Soviet Union also had nuclear power plants and nuclear weapons, but no crowds would ever dare assemble in Red Square to protest Soviet nuclear programs. In fact, the worst nuclear accident in history was in the region of the South Urals where the Soviet government built its first atomic reactor. The same area was used as a test site for a nuclear bomb in the winter of 1957. The explosion tore hundreds of pounds of radioactive waste from underground storage compartments, and radioactive dust was thrown more than six hundred miles. Five hundred innocent people died.

The government tried to cover up the incident and never made a public apology for this terrible disaster. Yet the Kremlin was always ready to criticize the nuclear policies of the West and condemn the Americans for being callous and inhumane.

"The operation against the imperialists' atomic plants failed," the chairman continued, "largely due to the actions of a mysterious five-man team. Our intelligence sources within the United States indicate this special unit was not working for the Department of Justice, the Central Intelligence Agency or the Federal Bureau of Investigation."

"You referred to them as a commando team," Major Shalnev, the paratrooper, remarked. "Perhaps they are part of the Green Berets or some other elite fighting unit."

"They're more than commandos," Colonel Kostov stated. "They're very professional intelligence and espionage operatives, as well. I know this for a fact, Major."

"Colonel Kostov and his assistant, Captain Igor Vitosho, were taken prisoner by an assault force that invaded another KGB operation on the Island of Krio off the coast of Greece," the chairman explained. "We recently traded four Jewish dissidents with the Greek government to have our Bulgarian allies returned to their homeland."

"Then you've seen these five supermen?" Major Potapov asked the Bulgarian.

"I held two of them prisoner," Kostov answered. "Briefly. They were very clever. Very professional. They called themselves Anthony Peters and Ramon Santos, but I'm certain those were cover names."

"They're Americans?" Shalnev frowned.

"One was a Caucasian and the other was Hispanic," the Bulgarian answered. "I'm not certain if they were Americans or not, but I imagine they were. The man with one hand who seemed to be their commander, now he was a European. I'm certain of that."

"European?" Colonel Burov snorted. "That doesn't help much, Comrade. What was he? French? German? Greek?"

"I'm not certain," Kostov said with a shrug. "His accent was barely noticeable and his English was flawless. I suspect he was raised speaking more than one language."

"This fits with what little we've been able to learn about the enemy," the chairman declared. "The one-handed man is middle-aged, nationality unconfirmed, but he apparently speaks at least three languages fluently, including Russian."

"What about the other four?" Shalnev inquired.

"A Hispanic of some sort," the chairman began wearily. "One is a Negro, tall with a mustache."

"*Chernozhopy*," Burov muttered, using the Russian term for "nigger," literally translated as "black ass."

"He might be a *chernozhopy*," the chairman snapped. "But you'd better not underestimate him. This is unit of highly skilled professionals. They didn't recruit the black one because affirmative action forced them to take him."

"*Da*, Comrade Chairman," Burov replied. "I'll take the little black monkey seriously, but I assume the other two are white. Correct?"

"Correct," the chairman confirmed. "One of them is a muscular man, probably American. The other is tall and lean, possibly British, although he could be American or even Australian. Apparently he can imitate other accents. We have to find these mysterious commandos, gentlemen.

We believe they've destroyed Soviet operations in the United States, Greece, Turkey and, most recently, in India.''

"Operation Postcard?" Major Potapov inquired.

"You should not discuss classified information!" Burov said sharply to the GRU officer.

"It's all right, Colonel," the chairman declared. "Operation Postcard is ancient history now. Exactly what was involved isn't important at this time, but I want you all to realize that the KGB, GRU and the Russian army were working together on that mission. Every single officer and soldier assigned to the base in India was butchered by these gansters."

"Five men couldn't have done that alone," Shalnev insited.

"Of course they've enlisted the assistance of others," the chairman answered. "Greek intelligence, Turkish Security Service, Indian CID and possibly the American CIA and National Security Agency on occasion. But make no mistake about this, in every case this team took command of the operation and carried out their mission with one-hundred percent success. A couple of early reports indicate that one of the commandos was an Oriental, possibly Japanese. We believe he may have been killed during a mission and replaced by the black man. However, as far as we know, this is the only casualty they've suffered thus far."

The chairman stood up behind his desk and stared at the other four men. "We, however, have suffered considerably more. Half-a-dozen KGB operatives are dead, at least one GRU officer and more than a dozen Soviet soldiers were also killed over the past three years. All killed by these imperialist machines of destruction. The failure of these missions has cost the Soviet government millions of rubles. Every loss we've suffered is a victory for our enemies. And this is why you have been summoned to my office, gentlemen."

"To find these commandos, Comrade Chairman?" Shalnev frowned. "But we don't know who they are."

"We've been collecting information about these men for three years, Comrade Major," the chairman told him. "But until now, we did not have an actual eyewitness to help us confirm the identity of any suspects who may be among the commando team. Now, with the help of Colonel Kostov and Captain Vitosho, I'm certain we'll be able to find at least one of the bastards. If you can find one, locating the others shouldn't be difficult."

The chairman of the KGB lowered himself into the leather armchair behind his desk. "And then you will hunt them all down, gentlemen," he concluded. "And terminate all five of them with extreme prejudice."

2

Five silent black shapes stealthily moved among the shadows surrounding a cluster of mango trees and giant ferns. Dressed in black night-camouflage uniforms, the five men were one with the darkness. Five stalking leopards who had located their quarry.

Colonel Yakov Katzenelenbogen, the unit commander of Phoenix Force, peered through the Starlite viewer. He braced the nightscanner with the tri-hook device at the end of the prosthesis attached to what remained of his right arm. The Israeli adjusted the light-density level to transform the moonless night into mere twilight. Katz aimed the viewer at the figures clustered along the shore approximately two hundred yards from the commandos' position.

A drab, battered old fishing boat floated offshore. Several figures waded to the vessel, towing a small rowboat through the water. Figures on board the boat lowered two oblong crates to the men on foot who guided the containers into the belly of the tiny craft.

Katz read the cyrillic letters stenciled on the side of the crate. He had no trouble understanding the Russian words. It was one of six languages Katz could speak, read and write fluently. He shook his head slightly, dismayed by the stupidity of the smugglers.

"The boxes are loaded with Kalashnikov assault rifles," Katz whispered to his nearest teammate. "It's written in Russian on the side of the crate. How's that for inconspicuous?"

"Especially in Puerto Rico," Gary Manning replied dryly as he slipped a NATO FAL rifle from his shoulder.

"Got us a bunch of real mental giants," Calvin James added. The big black man from Chicago eased his thumb along the selector switch of his M-16 assault rifle, but he did not flick it from safety to semi- or full-auto.

"The Arma de Liberación de Puerto Rico has never been considered very bright," Rafael Encizo whispered. "Even compared to other terrorist outfits."

"Well," David McCarter quipped, adjusting the 9-inch sound suppressor attached to the stubby barrel of his M-10 Ingram machine pistol, "we're about to put these blokes out of the gunrunning business for good. Everybody's good."

"Not theirs," Encizo commented. The muscular Cuban had taken a Heckler & Koch MP-5 from his shoulder and eased his hand around the pistol grip.

"Hell, mate," McCarter said with a grin, patting his trusty Ingram, "those buggers are so dumb they're better off dead."

"No shooting unless we have to," Katz reminded the battle-eager McCarter. "Let's try to take these fellows alive if they'll let us."

"I count fifteen guys on the shore," Gary Manning commented. The husky Canadian gazed through the Starlite scope mounted on the barrel of his FAL. "Probably at least five on board the boat. Figure they'll just surrender?"

"Sure wouldn't be typical of the ALPR if they do," Encizo added simply.

The Arma de Liberación de Puerto Rico had a well-deserved reputation for viciousness and total fanaticism. It was a pro-Castro terrorist group dedicated to achieving freedom for Puerto Rico. The ALPR's concept of "freedom" was to sever all ties with the capitalist Wall Street butchers of the United States and join hands with the progressive powers of Havana and Moscow. Like most terrorists, the ALPR were merely puppets of Communist subversives.

The ALPR had been active in the United States, where they had attempted a major hostage-taking and blackmail

scheme that went sour. A large band of terrorists seized
control of the Hillsdale Pacific Bank in San Francisco and
started making an assortment of outrageous demands. To
satisfy those demands the police sent in their Special Weapons and Tactics squad. Calvin James was a SWAT sergeant
at the time and he entered the building to discover two
members of Phoenix Force already inside, dealing with the
terrorists in a quiet, lethal and professional style. The incident ended in an enormous defeat for the ALPR and the
recruiting of Calvin James into Phoenix Force.

Now, more than a year later, the ALPR was conducting
terrorist actions in Puerto Rico. They had displayed their
hopes for "freedom and peace" by murdering five police
officers in San Juan and Ponce, firing a rocket launcher at
a military limo outside the San Juan naval station, and detonating a shrapnel bomb at a sidewalk café in Fajardo.

The ALPR was striking all over the island nation when
the problem came to the attention of the President of the
United States. The man in the Oval Office contacted Hal
Brognola, the control officer of Stony Man Operations.
Brognola assigned Phoenix Force to the mission. For the
most highly-trained team of international antiterrorists and
covert commandos in the world, the assignment was business as usual.

Phoenix Force had arrived in Puerto Rico aware of two
facts. First, someone among the local authorities had to be
feeding information to the ALPR terrorists in order for the
fanatics to stay one jump ahead of everyone chasing them.
Phoenix would not waste time trying to play who-do-you-trust with the Puerto Rican police. Secondly, the terrorists
were using Soviet-made weapons. This suggested the ALPR
was being supplied by Cuba, although the weapons might
be coming from Nicaragua or even Panama.

The Phoenix Force pros concentrated on questioning
various black marketeers and dope dealers, especially cocaine peddlers who were probably getting their nose candy
from Colombia. The illegal underworld merchants had to
acquire their goods from smugglers and nobody knows the

business like the competition. After squeezing some information from certain coke smugglers, Phoenix learned that the dope boys and other black marketeers avoided a certain cove near the shore of the Bahia de Guaynilla. This was an unhealthy area to do business because it was already claimed as the port of entry for some gunrunners who would not hesitate to kill anyone who dared to poke his nose into the cove's covert activities.

Phoenix Force staked out the cove for three days and nights. At last, the ALPR arrived at the shore to greet the fishing boat bearing gifts from their Communist comrades. The Cyrillic lettering on the crates being delivered left no doubt that Phoenix Force had found their quarry.

"Too bad this isn't television," Calvin James whispered. "Then we could just shoot up some sand, tell those dudes to throw down their weapons and nobody would get hurt."

"This isn't television," Encizo replied. "If we get canceled, we won't be back in reruns."

"Let's get to business," Katz told them, his voice soft but his tone sharp. "Fan out and form a horseshoe pattern so we can cover the bastards on three sides with the sea to their backs."

"What about the boat?" McCarter asked. "We're not going to just let them sail away, are we?"

"They might have machine guns or grenade launchers on board," the Israeli replied, unslinging his Uzi subgun from his left shoulder. "Taking the boat would be more risk than it's worth."

"Yakov is right," Gary Manning agreed. "Besides, those are just messenger boys bringing in AK-47 parcels. They're just carrying out the orders of their government. Blow 'em away and somebody else will be delivering guns somewhere else."

"Oh, shit," James muttered when he noticed a man on the bow of the fishing vessel with a pair of wide-lens binoculars raised to his eyes. "Is that what I think it is?"

"It's a Nochglaz," Katz answered. "A Soviet-made infrared scanner."

"Jesus," Manning rasped, raising the buttstock of his FAL rifle to his shoulder.

"¡Hijo de la chingada!" the man with the Russian night-scanner shouted, pointing at the mango trees where Phoenix Force was hidden.

Another sailor appeared at the port side with an AK-47 raised. He aimed the Soviet assault rifle at the trees and prepared to open fire. Manning triggered his FAL, and three 7.62mm rounds smashed into the chest of the smuggler gunman. His body hurtled back from the handrail as a shriek of agony burst from his lips.

Phoenix went into action. They quickly spread out to avoid giving the terrorists a single easy target. Several of the ALPR goons were already armed. Others drew knives from belt sheaths and used the blades to pry at the crates of newly arrived assault rifles. A man on the fishing boat emerged from the companionway with a Soviet RP-6 rocket launcher. He swung the Russian blast machine toward the mango trees.

"Kiss my black ass, boy," James growled, reaching for the M-203 grenade launcher under the barrel of his M-16.

James triggered the M-203 and the grenade launcher belched, jarring the rifle mount against James's hip with a recoil similar to that of a 10-gauge shotgun. The 40mm projectile caused more havoc than any burst of buckshot. The grenade exploded on impact and the high-explosive charge vaporized the smuggler with the RP-6 and smashed apart a portion of the hull of the fishing vessel.

Suddenly the entire boat erupted in a brilliant fireball. The second explosion hurled ALPR terrorists across the beach like tenpins. The wreckage of the fishing vessel was scattered across sand and water; some of the debris was burning, set afire by petrol tanks that went up with the explosion. Arms and legs floated among the remains of the enemy craft.

"Must have been hauling something pretty unstable," Gary Manning, the unit demolitions expert said. "Maybe those dummies were actually carting around straight dynamite and forgot to turn them. Nytro tends to seep into one spot and it—''

"Christ," McCarter snapped. "Save it for your bloody lecture tour, Gary."

The Briton turned his attention and the barrel of his M-10 Ingram toward a trio of ALPR flunkies who were still on their feet and armed with an assortment of full-auto weapons. McCarter opened fire. Nine millimeter parabellum rounds harshly coughed from the muzzle of the sound suppressor.

Two terrorists cried out and performed a macabre version of the jitterbug. Their death dance sent them into the sand where they twisted and convulsed briefly until all functions of life ceased forever.

The third ALPR enforcer caught two 115-grain flat-nosed slugs in his left arm. The bullets tore skin and muscle to shatter bone and the force spun the hapless terrorist around. As he pivoted, the gunsel triggered a Czech Skorpion machine pistol, firing a long burst of 7.65mm hornets into the chest of one of his own comrades. The ALPR goon's mouth fell open in astonishment as his breastbone was slammed into broken shards and his chest cavity transformed into a mangled collection of bullet-punctured sludge. He slowly slumped to the ground, lifeless eyes glaring at the comrade who killed him.

The wounded ALPR terrorist dropped to one knee and tried to swing his Skorpion back toward McCarter. Rafael Encizo promptly triggered his H&K MP-5. The West German chatterbox spat out a rapid 3-round burst that smashed into the terrorist's back, between his shoulder blades. The 9mm slugs shattered vertebrae and severed the fanatic's spinal cord like a taut thread. He fell face first in the sand, dead.

Two more ALPR warriors whirled toward Encizo and raised their AK-47s. The Cuban hit the dirt as twin streams of steel-jacketed 7.62mm rounds knifed through the air where he had stood. Encizo adopted a prone position, aiming his H&K at the terrorists and opening fire. Three 9mm messengers burrowed into the closest ALPR thug's lower abdomen, drilling through his guts like a trio of high-velocity awls. The man doubled up in agony as the other Puerto Rican low life lowered the aim of his AK-47 and prepared to squeeze the trigger. Encizo was faster. The Phoenix Force pro fired up at his opponent, and parabellum slugs split the terrorist's face and plowed through his brains.

Yakov Katzenelenbogen cut off the escape route of two fleeing ALPR gunsels. The Israeli braced his Uzi submachine gun across his prosthetic arm and fired a volley of 9mm destructors at the legs of the retreating terrorists. The pair tumbled to the sand, shrieking in pain and clawing at their bullet-shattered limbs. One idiot yanked a .38 revolver from his belt and tried to aim it at the Israeli.

"Adios," Katz whispered as he pumped a 3-round burst through the moron's chest.

Flecks of blood and torn skin splattered the face of the wounded terrorist. The man screamed in horror and abandoned his weapon as he clawed at the sand, dragging himself across the beach like an injured snake. Katz dashed from cover and ran toward the crawling figure. The man rolled over onto his back and prepared to throw a fistful of sand at the Isreali's face, but the Phoenix Force commander lashed out a boot and kicked the steel toe squarely against the point of the terrorist's chin. The man sighed, seeming to welcome the black veil of unconsciousness that descended upon him.

Gary Manning tracked the progress of two fleeing terrorists through the Starlite scope mounted on his FAL. The Canadian suddenly caught an abrupt movement out of the corner of his eye and whirled to confront a charging ALPR lunatic with a machete raised in a two-fisted grip.

The long blade of the jungle knife chopped down hard, struck the barrel of Manning's FAL and deflected the rifle toward the ground as the Puerto Rican killer slashed a crossbody stroke at Manning. The Canadian leaped away from the machete, but he was forced to release the FAL to avoid the sharp blade.

"¡Yanqui cochino!" the terrorist spat as he lunged, aiming the point of his jungle knife for Manning's belly.

The Phoenix fighter suddenly sidestepped and the machete stabbed air inches from Manning's right hip. The Canadian's hands flashed and swiftly snared the wrist behind the machete. He forcibly yanked his opponent forward and slammed a knee lift to the terrorist's gut. The ALPR slob folded at the middle with a choking gasp.

Manning quickly applied a straight-arm bar, a fundamental jujitsu technique that locked the terrorist's elbow with his arm fully extended. The Puerto Rican thug still held on to his jungle knife, so Manning did not pull any punches with the guy. He hammered the bottom of his fist into the terrorist's rigid elbow. Bone grated as the joint popped apart. The terrorist bellowed in pain.

The Canadian commando adroitly twisted his opponent's broken arm. The man howled louder than ever as Manning forced the guy's wrist up between his shoulder blades. The agony of this pressure to an already broken limb was too great and the terrorist uttered a helpless sob and fainted.

Manning almost felt sorry for the guy, but since the terrorist had tried to carve him up with a machete, the Phoenix Force pro figured sparing the ALPR goon's life was charitable enough. He dumped the terrorist to the ground and gathered up his FAL.

The two terrorists who had ran from the sights of Manning's rifle did not get far. Calvin James emerged from the cover of a mango tree and aimed his M-16 at the pair. He suddenly shifted the direction of his barrel and squeezed the trigger. Three 5.56mm projectiles plowed into the ground in front of the terrorists, and sand spat up, startling the ALPR goons into a full stop.

"¡Sus manos arriba!" James shouted, telling the terrorists to raise their hands.

One Puerto Rican mental case swung his Commie assault gun at the black commando. Calvin James fired his M-16 and sliced a vertical line of bullet holes in the gunman's chest from his breastbone to the hollow of his throat. The ALPR dude toppled over, dropping his AK-47 as he fell to the sand and thrashed around in a spasm of death.

"Don't you guys watch TV, man?" James said dryly as he slowly approached the other terrorist.

"*¡No, señor!*" the ALPR follower cried out, tossing his Skorpion machine pistol aside. "*¡Madre de Dios, no!*"

"Don't worry," James assured him, speaking the poorly accented Mexican-Spanish he had learned as a kid in Chicago. "I won't shoot you unless—"

The terrorist suddenly made a wild grab for James's rifle, and the former SWAT expert swung the M-16 beyond the reach of the ALPR dude's groping fingers. The black warrior turned with the motion and hooked a tae kwon-do kick to his opponent's right kidney. The man groaned as James's foot returned to earth. He immediately lashed out his other leg in a lightning-quick snap kick to the terrorist's stomach. The man gasped and started to double up, but James slammed a butt stroke to his face. The hard plastic smashed into the nerve line between jawbone and ear, and the terrorist dropped like a felled steer in a slaughterhouse. But unlike the steer, the Puerto Rican was still breathing.

"Come on, asshole," James muttered as he grabbed one of the guy's ankles and started to drag the senseless figure across the beach. "We don't have all night."

Several terrorists had been stunned by the the explosion when the fishing boat blew up. One ALPR zealot regained consciousness and slowly reached for his Kalashnikov, which lay less than a yard away. A boot stamped his wrist, pinning the terrorist's arm to the ground and he stared up to the black hole of the muzzle of Rafael Encizo's H&K blaster aimed at his face.

"*Buenas noches,*" the Cuban greeted.

"*¿Qui...quién es?*" the terrorist gasped weakly.

"*¿Queén soy yo?*" the Cuban grinned. "Who am I? I'm the hombre who will blow your head off unless you surrender, *chico.*"

"I surrender," the terrorist replied with an earnest nod.

3

Hal Brognola leaned back in his chair and puffed on the cigar. The tobacco was well cured and moist. The Fed had never smoked a Filipino cigar before, and it was a lot better than he figured it would be.

"Thanks again, David," Brognola told McCarter.

"Just happened to think of you when we were in the Philippines," the Briton replied with a wiry grin.

Brognola, the control officer of Stony Man, sat at the head of the conference table in the war room. The five men of Phoenix Force were assembled around the table. The Fed was thankful they had all returned in one piece from their brief mission in Puerto Rico.

Stony Man had originally been created to tap the incredible resources of combat expertise and battle experience of one man—Mack Bolan, better known as the Executioner. Bolan had stunned the world by his one-man war against the Mafia. The Executioner had accomplished the impossible. He had not only survived, he'd triumphed.

Bolan was chosen to head a new supersecret organization to combat international terrorism, and after taking on the cannibals of organized crime, he was ideally qualified to combat the modern-day vandals of terrorism. However, this was a worldwide threat that had more than one head. Even the Executioner could not fight terrorism alone.

In consequence, two special strike units were formed. Able Team consisted of three old friends and former allies of the Executioner in campaigns against the Mafia. Selecting the men for Phoenix Force had been more difficult. Bolan had personally made each choice, with the exception of Calvin James who was recruited by the commandos themselves.

For unit commander, Yakov Katzenelenbogen was perfect. Katz's experience in combat, espionage, intelligence and antiterrorist tactics began when the Nazis invaded France. Katz was the son of a noted linguist and translator, a Russion Jew who had fled to western Europe after the Bolshevik Revolution proved to be the preamble for another form of tyranny in Mother Russia. When most of the Katzenelenbogen family fell victim to Hitler's death squads, Yakov joined the underground resistance.

Katz later served with the OSS behind enemy lines, and by the end of the war he was a seasoned veteran of intrigue, urban warfare and sabotage. Later, Katz moved to Palestine and fought in Israel's war for independence. He saw more combat with Arab enemies of the Jewish state during the Six Day War, when Katz lost his right forearm on the battlefield. His only son was killed during the same incident, but Katz remained undefeated.

He became a member of Mossad, Israel's major intelligence network. Circumstances also allowed Katz to work with other intel organizations throughout the free world. The American CIA, the West German BND, the British SIS and the French Sûreté all benefited from the abilities and experience of the one-armed warrior. A better leader for Phoenix Force would be hard to imagine.

David McCarter's qualifications were almost as impressive. A former sergeant in Great Britain's elite Special Air Service, McCarter had participated in assignments to Northern Ireland and served as a "special observer" in Vietnam. He was later sent to Oman during the Omani Ohofar War in the 1970s.

The SAS war machine returned to England only to be assigned to a special covert police-action mission in Hong Kong. Following this clandestine operation, McCarter saw action in London itself when he was one of the SAS commandos selected for Operation Nimrod, the brilliant and highly successful siege of the Iranian embassy in 1980.

McCarter was a superb pilot and an excellent driver who once tested race cars for an occupation. He was also a champion pistol marksman and would have participated in the Olympics if the battlefields of the SAS had not taken him away from competition. Not that McCarter objected. He thrived on action and adventure. If he had less morality and patriotism, David McCarter would have become a professional mercenary or a gangster. As it turned out, he had exactly the right personality and talents for Phoenix Force.

Rafael Encizo's background was considerably different, but no less extraordinary. The Cuban had been a fighter since he was a boy growing up in Havana before Fidel Castro came to power. His family refused to accept the Communist regime and were slaughtered by Castro's troops. Encizo fled to the United States but returned among the Cuban freedom fighters during the disastrous invasion at the Bay of Pigs.

Encizo was taken prisoner and held at Castro's infamous El Principe prison. Starved, threatened and beaten, the Cuban warrior refused to betray his friends. The Communist torturers even used an electric cattle prod on Encizo, but still they could not break him down.

Then Encizo seemed to become less defiant. He appeared to be slowly weakening. The Communists rewarded him with more food and better treatment. He gave names and locations—which Castro's secret police would later learn were totally fictitious. The guards relaxed around Encizo, and this error cost one jailer his life. Encizo broke the guard's neck and successfully escaped from El Principe. He returned to the United States and became a naturalized citizen.

Stateside, the Cuban had numerous occupations. He worked as a scuba instructor, a professional bodyguard and even participated in a treasure hunt, diving for sunken Spanish gold. Encizo was working as an insurance investigator specializing in maritime claims when he was contacted by Hal Brognola. Fearless in battle and fiercely loyal to his teammates, Encizo was ideal for Phoenix Force.

Gary Manning was one of the best demolitions and explosives experts in the world. Like McCarter, the burly Canadian had served as a "special observer" in Vietnam where he was attached to the Fifth Special Forces and participated in several SOG missions in both South and North Vietnam, as well as one extremely dangerous assignment in Laos. Manning had always been a superb rifle marksman, an ability first developed while hunting deer in his native Canada. This skill served him equally well when he stalked men in Southeast Asia, and he became a deadly expert sniper, as well.

"If Manning can't shoot it down," one American NCO once remarked, "he'll blow it up."

Manning was awarded the Silver Cross, one of the few Canadian citizens to receive this decoration during the Vietnam conflict. He returned to Canada to be drafted into the intelligence section of the Royal Canadian Mounted Police. Thanks to a trade agreement with West Germany, Manning traveled to Europe where he served with the newly formed GSG-9, the Federal Republic of Germany's elite antiterrorist squad. Manning received firsthand experience with urban warfare and the European breed of terrorists who, Manning decided, were not much different from the Vietcong or the Pathet Lao.

When the RCMP were pushed out of the intelligence business following accusations of abuses of power, Manning turned to the private sector. He married and planned to have a family, but his workaholic nature soon ruined his brief marriage. Putting the divorce behind him, Manning concentrated on business and became a security consultant and a highly paid junior executive for North America International. But when he received an opportunity to once again battle terrorism with Phoenix Force, the Canadian dynamo eagerly accepted.

Calvin James, the newest and youngest member of the team, was a product of the mean streets of the south side of Chicago. He was already a veteran street fighter and knife artist before he joined the Navy at seventeen. James became a hospital corpsman with the elite SEALs, and like so many others Calvin James soon found himself in the Southeast Asian hell known as the Vietnam conflict. He saw plenty of action and emerged from the service with several decorations for valor.

Most important to James was the GI bill that he intended to use to continue his career in medicine and chemistry. However, his plans changed when his mother was killed by muggers and his younger sister died from a heroin overdose. James decided to become a policeman, and living in California he joined the San Francisco SWAT team. Phoenix Force recruited him to assist in a mission against the sinister terrorist conspiracy of the Black Alchemists, and James had remained with the unit ever since.

An expert frogman, combat medic and skilled ass kicker, James fitted into Phoenix Force as if he had been born for such a unit. Perhaps he had. The Force was five men, very different in many ways, yet so very much alike in their dedication to combat the enemies of freedom and civilization. They were the best, the very best in their profession. If the government, military and conventional intel organizations could not handle the task, Phoenix Force would get the job done.

Stony Man and Phoenix Force had survived numerous storms that could have dashed the whole organization on the rocks, and by far the most serious blow had occurred when the Executioner himself fell from grace. Bolan was framed for a political assassination by the KGB. Once again, the Executioner was a man alone. He was a renegade, hunted by virtually every law-enforcement and intelligence network in the world.

The President nearly disbanded Stony Man, but a national emergency required the unique skills and expertise that only Phoenix Force could supply. Stony Man and

Phoenix Force were still in business and business never let up for long. The KGB was a constant threat and there were always terrorist outfits that were "privately owned" but just as dangerous. Although battered and wounded by the long war with the Executioner, the Mafia was not dead and buried. It was slowly making a recovery. Some of its members had joined with elements of the Union de Corse, the Colombian syndicate and the Mexican Mafia to form a new international crime network, MERGE.

As if this was not bad enough, an Oriental organization similar to MERGE had also been formed. The Chinese Black Serpent Tong, the Japanese *yakuza* Snake Clan and the Mongolian New Horde had joined forces to create TRIO. Phoenix Force had clashed with both of these supercriminal networks in the past, most recently in the Philippines. There would almost certainly be rematches with all their former opponents in the future, and God only knew what other forms of animal man would be pitted against Phoenix Force.

But as McCarter once said, *If it was easy, anybody could do it.*

"Well," Brognola began, blowing a smoke ring toward the ceiling. "You fellas did your usual outstanding job in Puerto Rico. The ALPR is out of business, at least for now. Their little wave of terrorism ceased after you guys gave them a taste of their own medicine."

"We gave them a hell of a lot more than they could ever dish out," James declared, a trace of pride in his voice.

"Well, Hal," Katz began, lighting a Camel cigarette with his battered old Ronson, "do you have another mission lined up for us?"

"Not right now," Brognola answered. "We'll just wrap up this debriefing and you can go get some R & R. You guys deserve it."

"Hell," McCarter muttered. "That business with the ALPR was a bleeding cakewalk."

"You wouldn't say that if you almost got a machete in the gut," Gary Manning commented, sipping his third cup of coffee since he'd taken his seat at the table.

"Don't worry, David," the Fed assured McCarter. "You guys never get much time away from the front lines. Frankly, I don't know why you aren't all shell-shocked by now."

"I think that might be David's problem," Rafael Encizo said with a grin.

"I'll need to know where you'll all be in case we get another job for Phoenix Force," Brognola stated.

"Well," Encizo began, "Calvin and I have been wanting to get in a little more underwater training. Last few missions haven't had too much call for frogman techniques, but we need to keep up with it. Maybe we'll head down to Florida and—"

"Wait a minute, man," James interrupted. "When we were practicing training exercises off the coast of Florida last year we almost got eaten alive by a school of sharks."

"We can go somewhere else," the Cuban said with a shrug. "But you'll find sharks anywhere you find the ocean."

"Then we'll train in one of the Great Lakes," the black man told him.

"A lake?" Encizo frowned.

"Sure." James nodded. "Lake Michigan. Nice big body of water, plenty of room to practice anything short of underwater demolition and simulated attacks on large vessels. We can even raid a garbage scow if you want."

"Lake Michigan," Encizo said with a sigh. "You really want to train in Lake Michigan?"

"What's wrong with it?" the black man insisted. "Did you know Lake Michigan is the only one of the Great Lakes that doesn't extend into Canada? No offense, Gary."

"That's okay," Manning assured him. "You can have a lake all to yourselves, that's fine with me."

"And," James continued, "it is a well-known fact that there has never been a single shark attack in Lake Michigan."

"You were a SEAL, Calvin," Encizo said. "I didn't think you guys were afraid of sharks."

"I'm not afraid of sharks," James insisted. "But I don't like the idea of having one of those big ugly mothers chewin' on my ass. I don't mind taking that risk on a mission, man, but just once let's practice somewhere that won't be so risky to life, limb, and gonads."

"All right," the Cuban agreed.

"Great." James smiled. "Look, Lake Michigan extends along Chicago. I'll show you my old stomping ground, Rafael."

"I've already seen Chicago," Encizo told him.

"Not the Chicago I'm going to show you, my man," James replied, lifting his eyebrows suggestively.

"Okay," Brognola said, chewing on the butt of his Filipino cigar, "what about the rest of you fellas?"

"Personally," Gary Manning began, "I'd like to get up to my cabin in the woods for a while."

"That's in Canada, right?" Brognola asked.

Manning nodded. "You've got something like a forest here and there in the States, but nothing like what we've got in Canada, Hal."

The Fed nodded. "How about you two? Yakov? David?"

"I'm not expected back in England for a few days yet," McCarter commented. "Didn't expect this Puerto Rico business to be so easy. 'Course, I might be able to take off with Janis up the coast to Scotland for a day or two."

"Might be a good idea to wait, David," Katz remarked. "I have a feeling something is going to happen within the next forty-eight hours that will bring us all together for an assignment."

"Yakov," Brognola began, almost biting through his cigar. "Have you gotten some information that hasn't reached Stony Man yet? Perhaps from your sources with Mossad?"

"Nothing like that," Katz assured him. "I just have...well, I had a strange dream. Silly really."

"What sort of dream?" Brognola asked, surprised by Katz's statement. The battle-scarred Israeli was not the sort to fret about nightmares. He had lived through too many in reality to find dreams distressing.

"I feel a bit foolish," Katz admitted. "But I dreamed about a monster stalking us across the country. A beast with three wolf heads on stalklike necks, attached to the body of a huge bear."

No one laughed or snickered. Every man in the war room knew Katz well enough to appreciate the fact that he had a highly developed sixth sense for danger. Would it really be so remarkable if this uncanny ability even worked while he slept? It has been said people who had tickets on the Titanic canceled their voyage after dreaming about the ship sinking. Might Katz have actually had a premonition of danger?

"I'd be glad to have you fellas stay at my cabin for a couple of days," Manning offered. "I plan to do a little deer hunting, and if I don't find any venison on the hoof, we can always go fishing. The forest is a great place for escape-and-evasion exercises, too. If nothing comes up by the end of the week, we could all get together for some training missions."

"Thanks, Gary," Katz said. "I accept."

"I'll come along too, mate," McCarter added. "Make certain you don't drink all that Scotch whiskey by yourself."

"Shit," Manning laughed. "Everybody knows you're a Coca-Cola addict. We'll get a couple cases before we head up to the hills."

"Okay," Brognola said, crushing out his cigar in a brass ashtray. "You guys let me know where I can get hold of you if anything hot comes up. Meantime, enjoy yourselves. You earned it."

"Say, Hal," Encizo began. "Do *you* ever get a chance for any R & R?"

"Me?" Brognola grinned weakly. "No, I don't. But then, I don't get shot at, either. Now, haul ass out of here before I decide to break out the brooms and mops."

4

"Tea, Colonel?" Captain Georgri Mikailovich Myshko inquired, placing a silver tea tray with a pot and two glasses on Lieutenant Colonel Burov's desk.

"I would prefer answers," Burov muttered as he scanned the reports from the computer printouts sent by the information sector.

"Does that mean you don't care for tea at this time, Comrade Colonel?" Myshko asked, the corners of his lips turning up slightly.

"Pour the tea, Captain," Burov replied with annoyance.

Myshko was the colonel's aide. He was assigned to assist Burov, but in the KGB this also meant he was a potential spy and informer. No Communist system or any other totalitarian regime can function without back-stabbing finks. Informers are honored servants of the interest of the people. It is the safest way for a coward to seek promotion. Burov was not certain if Captain Myshko was a coward or not. The captain was a bootlicker, but that did not mean anything one way or the other in the KGB. Burov had tasted his share of foot leather, too. When one belongs to an organization that can fabricate charges and arrange executions without trials, one has to do a bit of bootlicking.

"The Bulgarians have not been able to identify any of the American gangsters the chairman is so concerned about?" Myshko inquired.

"Not yet," Burov answered. "Our computer people have tapped into the memory banks concerning records of virtually every known intelligence operative in American espionage—CIA, NSA, FBI—even the American Secret Service, which is there solely to protect the President. Still nothing.''

''Perhaps the agents involved were recruited from the American military,'' Myshko suggested. ''Didn't the CIA select talented personnel in this manner in the past?''

''They used to,'' Burov confirmed. ''But that was more than twenty years ago. Now the CIA likes college personnel and they even run advertisements in newspapers for people.''

''No country could be that stupid,'' the captain said in astonishment. ''How do they intend to maintain security when they recruit people in such a manner for their intelligence services?''

''America hasn't done very well in maintaining security,'' Burov said with a laugh. ''Remember their 'secret space-shuttle mission' that was broadcast on national television? A Washington newspaper even announced when a spy satellite was to be put into orbit for surveillance of our country.''

''America must be a very strange place,'' Myshko commented. ''You'd think with such terrible security we'd have no trouble getting information about this special unit of gangsters. Perhaps these men were never used as field operatives until they served duty for the mission in Greece.''

''*Nyet,*'' Burov replied. ''The chairman is convinced this team has been working together for at least three years. Your first suggestion seems more likely, Captain. Perhaps someone in American intelligence did recruit military or even police personnel. Or they may have gotten their people from outside the United States.''

''As we use the intelligence networks in the nations of our allies?'' Myshko inquired.

''Perhaps,'' the colonel answered. ''But if these five men have been working together on several missions, I don't think they're actively serving in the intelligence service of another nation of the West.''

"Not actively," Myshko began. "But they have been members of another country's covert department. *Da?*"

"*Da!*" Burov looked at his aide with surprise. "You may have steered us in the right direction to solving half of our problem, Captain."

"Half?" Myshko frowned.

"Finding these men is only half the problem," Burov explained, sipping his tea slowly. "Our mission is to terminate the lot of them. Killing such men won't be easy."

"I realize you are in command of this mission, Comrade Colonel," Myshko began. "And you have far more information at your disposal than I, but you'll be commanding elements of the GRU and some of the finest commando paratroopers in the Soviet army, as well as agents from the KGB. You'll have almost two-hundred men under your command, Colonel."

"Two hundred five to be exact," Burov replied.

"And you're worried about dispatching five troublesome American gangsters?" The captain shook his head. "I mean no disrespect, Colonel, but as soon as we locate these hoodlums you'll be able to crush them by sheer weight of numbers."

"If we can engage them in open combat," Burov agreed. "But we can't conduct a full-scale war in the heart of a major city. We'll only be able to use a portion of our strike force at a time and battle strategy will have to be carefully planned to suit the circumstances. Worse, many of Major Shalnev's commandos don't speak English, or at least don't speak it well enough to pass as anything except Russians trying to speak English. Regardless of their fighting skills, those soldiers will be more a liability to us than an asset unless we can engage the enemy in open combat. And I doubt that they'll oblige us by this condition."

"But isn't Captain Shatrov of the Morkrie Dela section going to assist us?" Myshko asked.

Burov's lips twisted with disgust. Morkrie Dela meant "wet work," with the "wet" referring to "blood wet." A more precise translation would be "work to which there is no other choice.'' Morkrie Dela was the KGB section specializing in assassination and kidnapping. In the days of the NKVD it was known as SMERSH, but the infamous Murder Inc. section had undergone a few changes over the years. Most of them simply changes of title.

The Morkrie Dela section consisted of killers, plain and simple. Not soldiers or espionage agents in the true sense, but professional assassins. They were murderers, carefully selected from psychological profiles of sick and twisted individuals who could still be used to serve the state. Captain Shatrov was a typical example of their breed. He was a sociopath and a psychotic, but very clever and good at what he did. In the United States, Shatrov would probably have become a serial killer, but in the KGB he was a ''servant of the people.''

''Da,'' Burov told Myshko. ''Shatrov will assist us, but I'm keeping him on a leash until we need him. The chairman also insists I take one of the Bulgarians on the mission.''

''Colonel Kostov, the war hero?'' Myshko asked.

''I don't think so,'' Burov replied. ''Kostov is too old for this sort of thing. That mission in Greece a while back is proof of that. He's lucky that he's regarded as such a glorious hero to the revolution for his past victories against the Nazis, otherwise he'd probably be shot. But he'll be allowed to retire and live out his years on a nice little government pension. Unfortunately, Captain Vitosho will accompany us. He's actually a Bulgarian paratrooper, not an espionage agent, so he'll be assigned under Major Shalnev.''

''Why does this distress you, Colonel?'' Myshko asked.

''Because I believe Vitosho is a bit unstable,'' Burov explained. ''He was humiliated by the defeat at Krio Island and he wants revenge on the people who ruined that operation. Vitosho may become careless. I'd rather not have him involved. Professional espionage has no place for personal grudges.''

"I'm certain the chairman knows what he'd doing," Captain Myshko assured the colonel.

"If this mission fails the chairman will not be blamed," Burov declared. "*I* will."

"But if it succeeds," Myshko said with a smile, "you will certainly receive a promotion, Colonel. Probably to major general."

"*Da*," Burov replied, thinking that failure would probably mean a firing squad—if he was lucky. Quick death by bullets would be better than years of misery in a Siberian gulag. "Let's see if our comrades in information have any news."

Burov and Myshko left the colonel's office and moved through the corridor to an antiquated elevator. The lift was like an oversized bird cage attached to thick cables. The cables had been replaced over the years, but the cage had remained more or less unchanged. Supposedly this was because the old lift was a bit of the past glories of the Lenin era, and it was kept for nostalgia. Burov suspected the true reason was because the iron cage discouraged conversations that might be subversive and saved the state the expense of having to install listening devices in the elevator.

Five stories later, the two KGB officers left the lift and headed down the hallway to a computer center in the information sector. The room was full of computer terminals, monitors and printout machines. Most were manufactured in the United States. Perhaps Lenin was right when he said, "When we hang the last capitalist, the fool will sell us the rope."

Computer technicians were busy operating keyboards and checking screens for the results of their labor. Burov was fascinated by high-tech machines, but they totally baffled him. He had once heard that in the United States ordinary Americans owned their own personal computers. Of course, he knew better than to believe this. Such an absurd claim was obviously CIA propaganda.

Burov was surprised to find Major Leonid Potapov in the computer room. The GRU officer snapped to attention when the colonel approached, and Burov glanced down at the authorization badge pinned to Potapov's tunic.

"That gives you permission to be inside KGB headquarters, Major," Burov declared, jabbing a finger against the badge. "But it does include certain restrictions. This area is one of them."

"Izveniti'yeh, Tovarisch," Potapov replied. "Excuse me, Comrade. This restriction was not explained to me by you, the chairman or the security personnel within this building. This was an oversight on my part, Comrade Colonel. I shall try to develop telepathic abilities to avoid such problems in the future."

"Insolence is a very dangerous character trait, Major—" Burov began, a vein throbbing angrily above his right temple.

"Colonel," Ivan Suslikov, the chief computer technician interrupted urgently. "Before you reprimand Major Potapov, you may want to know why he is here."

"Oh?" Burov raised his eyebrows. He knew from experience it was seldom wise to act with haste. "Very well, I'm listening."

"Major Potapov realized the trouble we've had trying to identify the American gangsters," Suslikov explained. "He suggested we check for individuals from other capitalist countries who have worked for American intelligence organizations. We have found four individuals who may be among the group you are looking for, Colonel."

"Indeed?" Burov began. "How curious, since Captain Myshko and I were just about to suggest that you do exactly that, Comrade Suslikov."

"Then you must agree it is a good idea, Colonel," Potapov said with a smile.

"Mozuht'bit," the KGB officer replied. "Perhaps. We'll see if it works. We'll also find out if the illustrious GRU actually dared to put an eavesdropping device in my office."

"GRU spying on KGB?" Potapov chuckled. "Well, they say turnabout is fair play, Colonel. However, I suspect your own organization is more apt to install secret microphones in your office. Standard practice for the KGB."

"Gentlemen," Suslikov interrupted. "I would rather you discussed such matters after you leave my sector. I have no desire to get in the middle of this debate."

"Of course," Burov agreed. "Please tell us what you have thus far, Comrade."

"We have individuals who fit the general description of the one-handed man who is alleged to be the leader of the American gangster team," the computer man explained, glancing at his notes. "According to our records, only two subjects seem likely. They're both the right age, build and have the expertise and language skills to be the man you seek."

"What about the others?" Burov asked.

"We came up with five whites, three Hispanics and two blacks," Suslikov answered. "Now, if we can get Colonel Kostov to help confirm identification, I think we can narrow these down a bit."

"I just hope it doesn't eliminate the lot," Burov snorted. "I want Vitosho to help identify the subjects, as well, just in case the colonel's cobweb-strewn memory is faulty. Besides, when two Bulgarians put their heads together it equals half a brain."

"I'll get them," Captain Myshko announced.

Less than an hour later, Colonel Kostov and Captain Vitosho sat at a computer viewing screen, examining the grainy faces of suspects produced from the KGB records of enemy agents. Both Bulgarians dismissed several individuals, but selected two others as likely possibilities and confirmed a third as definitely one of the American commandos.

"The two you're unsure of are the one-handed suspects," Colonel Burov noticed, checking the names on a list. "A German named Heinz Muller and an Israeli named Yakov Katzenelenbogen."

"There's a certain irony in that," Major Potapov mused. "Especially since their ages would make both men teenagers during the time of Hitler."

"Muller was never a Nazi," Kostov declared, recalling what he read from the computer files. "But he was a German soldier during World War Two. Served under Rommel in Africa. Awarded the Iron Cross for valor. After the war he became a professional mercenary. Specialized in fighting communism in the Congo during the sixties. Probably hired by both the American CIA and the British on more than one occasion. Lost his right hand during the Mau Mau uprising in Kenya. Speaks four languages fluently, including English and Russian."

"And this man is in America now?" Burov inquired.

"Supposedly running a survivalist school," Vitosho answered. "In other words, he's training zealots to kill."

"Like we do in Southern Yemen?" Potapov remarked dryly.

"Shut your mouth, Major," Burov commanded. His voice was low but the tone was hard. "What about the Israeli?"

"Katzenelenbogen's credits are quite remarkable," Kostov answered. "He's worked with most of the intelligence networks of the West and speaks half-a-dozen languages. Supposedly he retired from Mossad a few years ago and makes his living as a free-lance author, writing about archaeology, not espionage. He also acts as a go-between for certain business deals between the United States and Western Europe with Middle Eastern countries. Apparently he has friendly connections in Saudi Arabia and Egypt, as well as Israel. Extraordinary man."

"Jewish pig," Burov spat. "Why can't you give us definite identification of one of the men as the commando leader?"

"Because the photographs are terrible," the Bulgarian colonel replied. "The pictures are grainy, blurred and obviously quite old."

"*Nichi'vo,*" Burov said with a shrug. "It doesn't matter. We'll check both men and find out which is the person we seek. Is the Jew living in America, as well?"

"He recently became an American citizen," Kostov confirmed. "He formerly held dual French-Israeli citizenship. Of course, he's still an Israeli citizen, as well, but he doesn't spend much time in the Middle East. In fact, your sources knew very little about Katzenelenbogen's activities over the past eight years. The man clearly knows how to keep a low profile."

"We'll find him," Burov insisted. "And the German swine, as well. If we can't determine which is the right man, we'll simply kill them both. They're both enemies of the Soviet people, anyway."

"I wish we had found the identity of that slimy little spic," Captain Vitosho hissed. "I have a personal score to settle with that Spanish-speaking lump of shit."

"This is not a personal vendetta, Captain," Burov warned. "Another remark like that, and I'll see to it you don't accompany us on the mission. Now what about the man you both identified as a member of the gangster team? The one you're absolutely certain of?"

"He's a Canadian named Manning," Kostov replied. "Gary Manning. Formerly a lieutenant in the Canadian army, although he served with American Special Forces in Vietnam. Most of the information about the man was acquired through a double agent in the Canadian Security Intelligence Service. Manning had been in the intelligence section of the RCMP. However, he has supposedly retired and gone into an import-export business."

"But you're certain he's one of the men we're looking for?" Burov demanded.

"Da." Colonel Kostov sighed. He almost sounded as if he had hoped the computer check would have drawn a blank.

"Ochen korosho!" Burov declared with a cruel smile. "Now we can begin our mission. A mission that will end in the utter destruction of this damned American commando team."

5

Gary Manning's cabin was located in a remote forest in the northeast portion of the province of Saskatchewan. He also kept apartments in Toronto, Vancouver and New York City, but the cabin and surrounding forest was Manning's favorite getaway spot. The enterprising Canadian owned a great deal of real estate in the United States and Canada. He was, in fact, a millionaire, although he did not flaunt his wealth and only a handful of people realized how much Manning was worth in dollars and cents.

Manning figured that when and if he decided to retire, it would be to the forests of Canada. Like all men, Gary Manning was a paradox. He was a workaholic who had made a fortune and largely ignored it. He was an explosives expert and top demolitions man, yet he was actively involved with organizations that worked to protect the natural beauty of the Canadian woodlands from falling to the scythes of progress. And Manning was an expert in violence and mayhem, yet he loved peace and freedom.

Perhaps more than any other member of Phoenix Force, Manning seemed the least likely to belong to an elite commando unit. Yakov Katzenelenbogen and Rafael Encizo had both been involved in espionage and combat since they were teenagers. Neither man did it for the money, of course. Katz had a fortune in gold coins—a favorite form of financial security among the French—and he also had two or three Swiss bank accounts with plenty of cash and precious metals stored away. Encizo was part owner of some very valuable coastal property in both Florida and California.

However, both men had been involved in clandestine and commando operations for so long it was difficult to imagine either would retire except by death.

Calvin James, on the other hand, was a maverick. He had never really fit in anywhere until he was in Vietnam with the SEALs. The SWAT team in San Francisco was not quite unorthodox enough for James, and he had found a home at Stony Man. David McCarter was just short of being a social misfit. He had dedicated his life to acquiring abilities suited only for combat. James was trained in medicine and was a skilled chemist, but all McCarter knew or wanted to know was combat.

Katz, Encizo and James had all lost family members through violence. But the Nazis had not rounded up Manning's family for the slaughter. The Communists had not killed Manning's loved ones or tortured him in prison. Manning's mother had not been murdered and his sister had not died from too much heroin in her veins. None of these had happened to McCarter, either, but McCarter was a little nuts.

Yet, McCarter, like James, was born and raised in a tough, lower-middle-class neighborhood. Of course, Katz and Encizo had also endured harsh ordeals at an early age. None of this was true for Manning. He was the product of a middle-class family and most of the ordeals he had endured had been due to his own choosing.

However, Manning shared one thing in common with his teammates. He was fiercely dedicated to fighting the forces of barbarity and destruction, the enemies of freedom and culture. Regardless of his other abilities and skills, this was what Manning did best.

At the moment, Manning was not thinking about the war against evil and tyranny. He drove his Jeep Cherokee across the rugged dirt road that cut a crooked swath through the forest. The tough vehicle handled the uneven surface with ease and the twin beams of the headlights knifed through the darkness. It was only 7:00 P.M., but the supermarket in Cree closed at eight.

Cree was an obscure little town on the Cree River. Most of the residents were Indians who minded their own business and expected everybody else to do the same. However, Cree had an honest-to-God supermarket, probably to cash in on vacationers and campers more than to serve the needs of the community. Of course, anything that attracted more business was welcome in Cree. The residents minded their own business, but they preferred it when business was good.

Manning pulled into the parking lot of the Cree Market Center and killed the engine. He left the Cherokee and turned up the collar of his sheepskin jacket to protect his neck from the crisp autumn breeze. Manning was unaware of the malevolent eyes that followed him across the lot.

"I thought that yellow Jeep belonged to you, Mr. Manning," Boris Shatrov said with a smile as he lowered his Night-Eye infrared binoculars. "This is almost too good to be true. If I believed in God, I'd thank him for delivering this Canadian swine to my doorstep."

After considerable effort, the Soviets had managed to track down Manning and learned he was in the northeast part of Saskatchewan, probably vacationing at his cabin. Shatrov and a team of Morkrie Dela agents under his command had checked into the Cree Hotel directly across the street from the market. The opportunity seemed like a godsend, even to an atheist like Boris Shatrov.

"How shall we handle this, Comrade Captain?" Dimitri Lagunin inquired. "I am an excellent marksman, as you know. I'm certain I could shoot the pig between the eyes as soon as he steps out of the store."

"No!" Shatrov said sharply. "We want this one alive so he can tell us where to find the other capitalist gangsters we seek. We must be careful. Manning is a professional. He'll recognize an obvious trap and we're not certain if he's armed."

"What shall we do?" Lagunin asked, patting the walnut stock of the Remington M-788 rifle that he dearly wished to use.

"Tell the others to get in here," Shatrov declared. "I think I know how to lure Manning into a trap. Tell them to be quick. We haven't much time."

Lagunin nodded, placing the rifle on the bed.

"After you finish that task," Shatrov continued, "I want you to put a sound suppressor on that rifle. The telescopic sights are infrared, correct?"

"Indeed, Comrade," Lagunin said with a smile. "Then you may want me to shoot the bastard after all?"

"Only as a last resort," the top assassin replied. "We want Manning alive, but we don't want him to get away. Better he's dead than escape to warn the others."

Lagunin agreed eagerly.

MANNING EMERGED from the Cree Market Center with a case of Coca-Cola and a bag of groceries and other household goods. He was heading for the Cherokee when a young woman hurried toward him. The three-inch high heels of her boots clicked against the pavement as she approached.

She was a real eyeful. A stunning blonde with shoulder-length hair, she was sexy enough to make a bishop decide celibacy was bullshit. The lady had a great body and she displayed it beautifully. Large round breasts strained the thin silk of her blouse. The woman's rabbit-fur coat was unbuttoned, the hem touching midthigh. A black leather miniskirt was about three inches shorter.

"Excuse me, Mister," she said, a trace of desperation in her voice. "I hate to bother you…"

"Bother me," Manning invited with a smile. "I don't mind a bit."

She smiled in reply. "Well, my car won't start," the woman explained. "Do you know anything about engines or whatever? I'm afraid I'm lost already and now this happens…"

"I'll take a look at your car, Miss…?"

"Just call me Sharon," the woman replied.

Manning opened the Cherokee long enough to stuff his groceries inside. Then he followed the woman across the lot, admiring the slight sway of her backside. Sharon walked toward a trio of cars parked in an unlit corner of the lot. Manning frowned when a notion forced its way into his mind.

Sharon had not been in the supermarket when Manning was shopping. He certainly would have remembered her if she had been. If she just pulled into the lot, how did she know her car would not start? Of course, there were a dozen possible explanations, but only one that might mean danger.

What if the woman was a lure?

"Oh!" Sharon exclaimed as her purse slipped from her shoulder and fell to the pavement.

As she bent over to retrieve it, her legs remained straight, allowing her coat and skirt to hike up to reveal a glimpse of silk panties. But Manning was not watching. He glanced in all directions. If the woman was supposed to distract him, that meant the real threat lurked somewhere else.

He saw it. A figure rose between a Buick and a station wagon, a large pistol held in a two-handed grip. Manning instinctively ducked. The pistol hissed like a serpent and something tugged at the collar of Manning's jacket. He ignored the near miss and bolted for the cover of a Chevy sedan.

A second projectile sizzled and scraped the trunk of the sedan as Manning ducked behind the vehicle. The second shot had come from a different direction. So there were at least two gunmen to deal with. The woman was a "swallow," a seductress who used beauty and sex as weapons. She would not indulge in physical combat unless it was in a bedroom. The blonde had already darted to cover and left the fighting up to her comrades.

Manning realized something was stuck to his collar. He tugged on the jacket and stared down at the feathered end of an object lodged in the sheepskin. The Canadian pulled it out and examined the dart. It was a tranquilizer dart, the type generally used to put big game animals to sleep in order to bring them back alive. Manning had used such darts on several occasions himself.

Of course, the sleep dart might be loaded with cyanide or some other liquid poison. But whether his opponents wanted him dead or alive, the situation was just as dangerous either way.

Manning did not intend to stay in one place. He shuffled to the front of the sedan and scrambled around the nose of an old pickup truck. He stopped, trying to tune out the thumping of his pounding heart as he strained his ears to detect any telltale sounds of his mysterious opponents. The Canadian heard a soft patting sound that could have been rubber soles against pavement. A slight electrical crackle may have been static from a two-way radio.

Don't jump to conclusions, he told himself. Jump the wrong way, you're dead.

Manning considered his defensive capabilities. He had not brought a gun to go shopping. There was a .357 Colt revolver hidden in a secret compartment under the seat of his Cherokee, but that would not help at the moment. The explosives expert always carried something that could "go boom" in an emergency. A grenade or two would have been ideal, but all Manning had was a few pencil detonators in the pocket of his shirt, and the money belt around his waist contained a thin strip of C-4 plastic explosives.

Suddenly, a figure rose alongside the pickup. The man, dressed in a navy blue jacket and hunting cap with rabbit-fur earflap, held a bulky pistol in his fists. Manning dropped to the pavement as the gunman's weapon hissed. A dart whistled over the Canadian's head, brushing his hair before it crash-landed on the pavement.

The Morkrie Dela agent worked the pump action of his air pistol, building up needed air pressure and chambering another dart from the magazine in the buttstock. Manning did not give him a chance to complete this task: the Canadian charged while his opponent was still fumbling with the weapon.

The Russian tried to point his air gun at the attacking figure, but Manning's hand caught him under the wrist and shoved the pistol toward the sky. The KGB hitman pulled the trigger and fired a harmless dart at the stars as Manning's right fist punched the killer in the solar plexus. The Canadian folded his knee and whipped it between his opponent's legs.

The Morkrie Dela moved a thigh to protect his genitals, and Manning's knee struck the firm muscle. The Russian grunted and hooked his left fist to the side of Manning's jaw. The Canadian's head barely moved from the punch, but the KGB man smoothly followed through with a kick. His boot struck Manning under his ribs, driving the breath from the Phoenix warrior.

The Russian swung his right fist, trying to hammer the butt of his air pistol on Manning's head. Manning raised a forearm to block the attack, and the killer's wrist struck the solid bar of muscle as Manning scooped his other arm around the side of his opponent's chest. The Canadian turned sharply, ramming a hip into the Russian's gut. With a hard twist, Manning sent the killer hurtling over his hip.

The gunsel slammed onto the steel body of a Ford Galaxy. He gasped as the impact jarred the fight from him. Manning quickly grabbed the Russian's hair and pulled his head forward to hammer a knee to the guy's face. Blood spurted from the assassin's nose and he began to sag. Manning could not afford to take any chances with his opponent. The Phoenix fighter seized the dazed Russian by the back of the belt and hauled him headfirst into the side of the pickup. The ugly crunch and liquid splat of the man's skull splitting open made Manning's stomach knot.

Two more figures rushed toward Manning's position, both armed with tranquilizer pistols. The Canadian ran, his back hunched and his head low. He heard or thought he heard one of the pistols hiss, however no dart struck Manning or came close enough for him to notice. He kept running, jogging between vehicles, trying to prevent his opponents from getting a clear shot.

He plucked a pencil detonator from his pocket and thumbed the dial. Manning had no idea what he set the timing mechanism for, but he dropped the detonator and kept moving. He ducked behind a Toyota Land Rover when he heard the firecracker bang of the pencil detonator exploding.

Manning glanced up from his shelter and saw that the two men who were chasing him had split up. Each man was on opposite sides of a Cutlass Supreme, and both had turned to stare at the sudden burst of light from the exploding detonator. Their backs were toward Manning.

The Canadian took a deep breath and charged forward. He leaped onto the hood of the Cutlass and used it as a springboard to dive toward one of the Russians. The startled KGB killer raised his pistol, but Manning pounced onto him as the air gun coughed. Both man fell to the ground, Manning on top. He pinned the attacker with his knees and smashed a fist into the man's face. Manning hammered the bottom of his fist onto the bridge of the bastard's nose and prepared to drive the heel of his palm under the nose to send broken shards of cartilage through the sinus into the brain.

Suddenly the other gunman dashed around the rear of the Cutlass, a pistol in his gloved fists. Manning hastily seized his dazed opponent and rolled to the right, pulling the stunned man with him. The second Russian fired his weapon and a steel dart struck the KGB operative who was now on top of Manning. The guy yelped with pain when the needle point pierced his flesh, and Manning shoved him aside.

"Sveeniya!" the assailant still on his feet snarled as he stomped forward and launched a kick at Manning's face.

A Russian, the Canadian thought as he jerked his head away from the slashing boot and the kick struck his shoulder. The force knocked Manning on his back and the attacker swung another kick and simultaneously worked the pump action of his air pistol.

Manning's hands snaked out and caught his opponent's ankle. He twisted the gunner's leg, nearly throwing the guy off-balance. The man staggered and hopped on one foot, trying to aim his pistol at the Canadian. Suddenly Manning shot up from the ground, driving the top of his hard skull between the KGB man's splayed legs.

The Russian uttered a high-pitched squeal as the ruthless head butt smashed into his sex machine. The force hurtled the trigger man against the hood of the Cutlass, and he slid along the smooth metal until he fell by the front fender. Manning dashed after him as the Russian started to rise, one hand still holding the tranquilizer gun while the other clutched his battered genitals.

Manning's boot kicked the pistol from his opponent's grasp, and the Russian uttered an ugly growl and launched himself at the Phoenix pro, hands aimed at Manning's throat. The Canadian's fist rose between the KGB man's outstretched arms, hitting the enemy agent with a powerful uppercut that lifted the Russian off his feet. The Kremlin killer flopped against the hood of the car, and his unconscious body slumped to the pavement, blood oozing from the corner of his mouth.

"Damn you!" Boris Shatrov swore through clenched teeth as he watched the battle through his Night-Eye binoculars. The Morkrie Dela boss grabbed his transmitter and switched it on. "Backup Two and Three, do you read me?"

"Backup Two," the voice of an operative in the parking lot replied. "Read you, sir."

"Backup Three," Dimitri Lagunin's voice answered. "Read you clearly, Comrade."

"Terminate subject immediately," Shatrov ordered.

6

"Do'svee daniyah," Dimitri Lagunin whispered as the cross hairs of his Night-Eye scope formed an *X* on Manning's forehead.

The Russian marksman was positioned on the roof of the hotel, sprawled prone with the buttstock of the Remington M-788 snug against his shoulder. Lagunin had never fired the rifle, but he had used similar weapons on other missions. The Morkrie Dela hit squad were all armed with American-made weapons to avoid a direct link to the Soviet Union.

Lagunin squeezed the trigger as Manning began to move to a different location. The KGB killer knew he missed as the recoil rode from the rifle into his shoulder. A big .308 smashed into the windshield of a Volkswagen behind Gary Manning. Glass shattered and a spiderweb pattern of cracks stretched across the window. The foot-and-a-half-long silencer attached to the barrel of the Remington reduced the report to a harsh rasp, but the broken windshield would certainly alert the quarry to danger.

"Holy shit," Manning muttered when the windshield exploded. "These people mean business."

As the Canadian dodged from car to car, he glimpsed three more gunmen advancing rapidly on foot. One of them raised a black pistol with a full-barrel silencer. Manning dived behind a green van as the pistol hissed softly. The Phoenix Force pro figured his opponents were probably armed with .22 Long Rifle caliber pistols. Good choice for close-range, silent work. The guy with the rifle was obviously armed with something a lot larger than a .22-caliber. Probably a bolt-action rifle. A sniper does not need rapid-fire if he is good enough with his weapon.

Whoever was hunting Manning, they were damn good. But they obviously did not want to attract too much attention in a public place—and that was on his side. Of course, if they decided that effort was a lost cause, they might blow up the whole parking lot if they wanted Manning badly enough.

"Let's see who blows up what first," the Canadian whispered as he slid the belt from his trousers.

He unzipped the pouch at the inside of the belt and peeled off part of the C-4 strip. He estimated the portion to be about a quarter of a pound. That should be enough, he hoped. Manning dropped to his belly and rolled on his back to wiggle under the van. He crawled with his heels and elbows until he was beneath the engine block. Manning groped inside and found a place to set the charge.

"Backup Two and Three," Shatrov spoke into his radio. "I cannot see the subject. Have you located him?"

"Nyet, Tovarisch...." a voice answered.

"Speak English, you idiot," Shatrov snapped.

"No, sir," the voice repeated sheepishly.

"I cannot see the subject, either," Lagunin stated. "I think he may have crawled under one of the vehicles."

"Seems logical," Shatrov agreed. "Search under vehicles in the area where you last spotted him, Backup Two, be careful. Backup Three, be ready to handle the subject if he bolts from cover."

"Yes, sir," Laguinin assured his commander, gazing through the infrared scope.

Suddenly Manning appeared at the rear of the van. Lagunin swung his rifle toward the Canadian and two of the pistolmen on foot charged. Manning dashed between an aisle of cars, slipping off his sheepskin jacket as he ran. The pistolmen fired two hasty shots at the fleeing figure. Lagunin held his fire until the cross hairs found the jacket. He squeezed the trigger. The silencer served as a flash cover, protecting the marksman's eyes from the muzzle-flash that would otherwise be painfully bright with the infrared sights. He saw the bullet hole appear in Manning's jacket before he realized the Canadian was not wearing it.

"Damn!" Lagunin snapped, working the bolt action to eject the spent cartridge casing and chamber a fresh shell.

He peered through the scope, slowly scanning the lot, hunting for his target. The two bolder KGB pistolmen continued to chase Manning, but the Canadian quickly ducked behind a vehicle, dropped to his belly and covered his head with both arms.

The van exploded, and the blast tore one of the KGB agents apart. Chunks of the Russian's body hurled in all directions. Metal and glass from the demolished vehicle became flying shrapnel and sharp shards hammered into the torso of the second pistolman like a monstrous burst from a blunderbuss. The multiple projectiles struck with such force that the Russian was hurled seven feet before his bloodied, mangled corpse crashed to the pavement.

Lagunin screamed, dropped his rifle and covered his eyes with both hands. The brilliant flash of the explosion had been amplified by the infrared scope. The Morkrie Dela sniper was certain his eyeball had burned out of its socket. The same thing happened to Captain Shatrov who had been watching the battle through his Night-Eye binoculars. The KGB team leader fell to his knees in the hotel room, moaning in pain as his eyes seemed to boil inside his head.

"Control, this is Backup Two," a voice announced from the transceiver. "Control, do you read me?"

Shatrov groped toward the sound, his vision still filled with the glare of the explosion. His hand fumbled along the nightstand by the bed until he finally found the radio. Shatrov switched the transmit button.

"Backup Two, this is Control," he said in a strained voice.

"Control?" the Russian henchman asked. "Are you all right, Control?"

"That damn explosion almost blinded me," Shatrov answered. "Did that...subject get away?"

"I'm afraid so, sir," the voice answered. "At least one of my men was killed and—"

"Backup Two?" Shatrov asked, afraid Manning may have sneaked up behind his agent and strangled him.

"I just saw the subject's Jeep pull out of the lot," the voice announced. "He's getting away, sir."

"Ya n'yeh mogo vid'yet!" Lagunin's voiced cried from the radio. "I cannot see!"

"You cannot think, you fool!" Shatrov replied angrily. "Speak English. The same thing happened to me when the explosion occurred. It will pass in a minute or two."

"Control, what shall we do now?" Backup Two wanted to know.

"Get back to base," Shatrov instructed. "We'll decide what to do then."

GARY MANNING TRAMPED the gas pedal as he drove the Cherokee away from the Cree Market Center. He took the .357 Magnum from its compartment as he worked the wheel with one hand. The Jeep sped across the dirt road into the forest, but Manning knew he could not drive back to the cabin.

Whoever his opponents were—and he had a pretty good idea—they knew enough about Manning to have a general idea where he was. They probably would not learn the exact location of the cabin. Manning owned twenty square miles of the Saskatchewan forest and only six people knew the exact site of his cabin. However, if his enemies were adept at tracking, they might follow his tire marks all the way home. This was unlikely, but it was probable that they had planted a tracking device in the Jeep. Perhaps more than one. The bastards were professionals. Manning could not rule out the possibility.

He chose a hard patch of land along the shoulder of the road, pulled over and parked the vehicle. Manning stuck the Magnum in his belt and locked up the Jeep. Then he jogged into the forest. Among his other talents, Manning was a long-distance runner. His endurance, physical and mental, was extraordinary. The Phoenix warrior ran through the woodlands at a steady pace, aware he could cover more ground by running slowly for a long time than by sprinting short distances and wearing himself out after the first mile.

He carried a flashlight but seldom used it. Manning knew the forest well and he had traveled on foot through it after dark before. His easy pace allowed him to cope with low hanging branches and jutting tree roots as he jogged in a wide circle, avoiding a direct route to the cabin.

Manning purposely selected hard ground when possible, aware he would leave fewer prints. He jogged to a cluster of trees and rested for a moment before reaching for the lowest strong branch. The Canadian climbed up the trunk and slithered along a thick limb to climb into another tree. He reached a third and swung down to the ground.

"Unless you bastards have a bloodhound that ought to take a while to figure out," he muttered as he continued to run.

At last Manning approached the cabin. He advanced slowly, revolver held in his fist. The lights were on inside and he saw no evidence of forced entry or violence. As he crept closer, the front door creaked open. A familiar figure stood at the doorway, an Uzi submachine gun canted on his left shoulder.

"Gary?" Katz called softly.

"Yeah," the Canadian replied with a sigh of relief. "Is everything okay here?"

"Everything is fine," Katzenelenbogen assured him. "Except David and I were beginning to get a bit worried about you. You've been gone an hour longer than you planned."

"Why the hardware?" Manning asked as he entered the cabin. "Never mind, silly question."

"We always feel better when we're armed," David McCarter answered, standing in the front room with his Ingram slung over his right shoulder and the Browning

Hi-Power in a holster under his left arm. "You look like hyou've been through a bit of a wringer, mate."

"You might say that," Manning replied. "I damn near got killed back in Cree. It was a professional setup and I think I know who they are."

"Start at the beginning," Katz instructed. "But give us an edited version if time is crucial."

"I'm not sure how much time we have, Yakov," Manning explained. "I'm pretty sure the KGB tried to kidnap me, and when that didn't work they tried to kill me. They had tranquilizer guns, silenced pistols, a sniper on the roof and a swallow in a miniskirt...."

"My kind of birdie," McCarter grinned.

"Funny," Manning grunted. "One of them muttered something as he was trying to kick my head in. I'm not sure, but it sounded like it was probably a rude remark in Russian."

"The fact that someone tried to kill you is enough," Katz said. "We'll have to assume they're after everyone in Phoenix Force and they're on their way here now."

"How lucky for them," McCarter stated. "They'll get to find three members of Phoenix Force. Let's arrange a nice reception for the bastards."

"Hold on, David," Katz urged. "All of us would like to stand our ground and fight, but this isn't the time for it. We don't know whether these people are after Gary, the three of us or all of Phoenix Force. As I said before, we have to assume the latter. That means we have to warn the others. If the KGB is responsible, they're perfectly capable of launching more than one hit team at multiple targets."

"Damn it," Manning muttered. "I thought Stony Man was supposed to be so goddamn secure. How did they find out about us...or least about me?"

"Never underestimate the opposition," the Israeli replied. "Whatever else you can say about the Soviet intelligence organizations, they are very efficient and very clever. Frankly, I'm not surprised this has happened. It was only a matter of time before the Kremlin started to put enough pieces together to come up with a general idea about Phoenix Force.''

"I hope it's just a general idea," McCarter said as he frowned. "If the Russians have enough details about us we're finished."

"For now we'd better concentrate on survival and trying to save the others before the sons of Beria find them," Katz declared.

"Beria?" Manning asked with confusion.

"Laverenti Pavlovich Beria," Katz explained. "He was the head of Soviet state security under Stalin. Beria was to the NKVD what Himmler was to the gestapo."

"Are we going to play Trivial Pursuit or get our arses in gear?" McCarter asked, rolling his eyes toward the ceiling.

"First I want to hear more details about what happened to Gary," Katz replied, unruffled by McCarter's outburst. The other members of Phoenix Force were accustomed to the Briton's temperament. He always got a bit anxious and short-tempered before they went into combat. "But you might get your gear together."

"Yeah. And I've got a Chevy pickup out back," Manning said. "You might start it up. I abandoned the Cherokee just to be safe."

"Bloody hell," McCarter complained. "I suppose you didn't get the Coca-Colas?"

"We'll pick some up on our way out of here, David," Katz said, shaking his head. "*If* we get out of here."

SERGEANT VIILOV GAZED AT A SCREEN on a device that resembled a metal detector. The machine was a highly sensitive heat-sensing device. The sergeant was a commando from Major Shalnev's elite paratrooper unit. Most Soviet soldiers below the rank of officer are not even trained to use maps, but Shalnev's troops were taught to handle a variety of unusual devices and weapons.

"He is very clever," Viilov stated. "He chose the rocky areas because they leave fewer footprints, but the stones absorb more heat."

"Are you certain this is his track and not someone else's?" Dimitri Lagunin asked with a frown. "This is miles from where he abandoned his Jeep."

"He ran," Viilov answered. "Ran many miles. But I am sure this track is his. The pattern of the heat from his boot soles is unmistakable."

"That's remarkable," Lagunin stated, awed by the machine.

"It's not really much different from the color body-heat photography that has been done by the Americans and the British for more than ten years," Viilov told his Morkrie Dela supervisor. "Ultraviolet light detects many kinds of color unseen by the naked eye. Every living object radiates heat and the heat can be contracted by inanimate objects such as a floor or the ground. Of course, this heat detector won't work in a warm climate and it would be totally useless in a desert. However, the ground and everything in this forest is cool this time of year, and the fact that we're working at night helps, too."

"I don't care to hear an entire lecture on the damn device," Lagunin said, bored with the discussion. He wished Comrade Shatrov had not put him in command of the unit to track down Manning.

This time the Canadian gangster would not escape. If they could find their quarry, the battle would be strictly one-sided. Lagunin had four Morkrie Dela assassins and ten Soviet paratroopers under his command. Fifteen to one was certainly formidable odds. Gary Manning was as good as dead the moment they found the bastard.

Comrade Shatrov had told Lagunin to capture Manning alive if possible. Bullshit, as the Americans would say. Lagunin would order the Canadian shot on sight. Manning was a fanatic. Lagunin had heard about such crazed mercs before. The man was an explosives expert. He would probably rig some sort of booby trap and try to blow himself to bits and take as many Soviets with him as possible. One does not take chances with such a man.

"The image is getting faint, Comrade," Viilov declared, checking the scanner. "The prints are cooling rapidly, and soon we will not be able to track him."

"If only we knew where that damn cabin was," Lagunin said helplessly, glancing over his shoulder at the thirteen other members of the strike unit. They were all armed with automatic weapons, side arms and knives. The Morkrie Dela killers were not trained for open combat. They were specialists in murder, not fighting an opponent on equal terms. However, the paratroopers *were* trained for such warfare. They were superb fighting men. They would send the devil back to hell...if only they could find Manning.

"Wait a minute," Sergeant Viilov said. "I think I found something."

He pointed the heat detector at a cluster of evergreens. The commando approached quickly, gazing at the multicolored patterns on the screen of his device.

"He climbed a tree," Viilov said with admiration for his wily quarry.

"He's up there now?" Lagunin demanded, raising his Remington rifle to gaze through the infrared scope.

"I doubt it," Viilov replied, moving farther into the forest. "Manning probably did this to make it more difficult to read his signs. If I were the Canadian, I'd move from tree to tree until I'd covered as much area as possible."

"That could only be two or three trees," another Russian commando declared.

"Da," Viilov agreed. "Now to find the right tree...."

He moved the scanner toward the base of a tree trunk. Viilov smiled. "Here it is," he announced. "Manning continues to move north. Clever. He thought his tactic would throw us off He may have succeeded if we did not have this heat scanner."

"You're doing a fine job, Sergeant," Lagunin assured him. "Now, if we can keep tracking that damned gangster, we'll find his secret lair and annihilate him. Bear in mind, all of you, this man is very dangerous and resourceful. Three of our comrades have already been killed."

"It must be a terrible blow to the ego of the KGB," Viilov commented, "to plan an assassination that turned out so badly."

"Watch your tongue, Sergeant," Lagunin snapped.

"You are in command for now, Comrade." Viilov smiled. "But you'd better leave Manning to us when we find him. Your Morkrie Dela tactics failed. But do not fear. The Soviet army will accomplish what you cannot."

"Just find Manning," Lagunin muttered, unable to dispute Viilov's claim. "Find the Canadian pig and kill him."

7

A bell chimed harshly inside the cabin and a red light flashed on in every room of the structure. Manning rushed to his den and yanked open the cabinet doors to a compartment in a large walnut bookcase. Inside sat a control panel of switches and dials mounted beneath a television monitor. The Canadian switched off the alarm.

"Red alert," Manning explained to Katzenelenbogen and McCarter. "The security system surrounding this place has been activated."

"We're under attack?" Katz inquired, slipping into a shoulder-holster rig. He raised the prosthesis until he could get the leather pocket containing a SIG-Sauer P-226 pistol in postion under his right armpit.

"Not necessarily," the Canadian replied. "Keio Ohara helped install this system. It's activated by any large moving object that breaks the electromagnetic field surrounding the cabin in a diameter of five hundred yards. It's invisible, but it works beautifully. Last summer it went off when a grizzly approached the cabin."

"I think this time it's the great Russian bear," McCarter commented. He turned to Katz, recalling the Israeli's dream. "A bear with three wolf heads."

"Sometimes I amaze myself," Katz said with a shrug.

"This is a pretty sophisticated system," Manning began as he threw two switches. "But Keio tried to keep the control panel simple. I just hope everything is in working order. I don't know how the hell I can get any of this stuff repaired without Keio."

Keio Ohara had been one of the original five members of Phoenix Force. A tall, pleasant and very intelligent Japanese, Ohara was an electronic wizard. His expertise and assorted skills still seemed to reach out from the grave to assist Phoenix Force from time to time. Ohara had been one hell of a man and his death had been the greatest blow the unit had ever suffered.

"Okay," Manning remarked when the TV screen turned from dull green to bright blue. "The land-sonar screen is working."

Several white blobs advanced from the edges of the screen. The shapes completely surrounded the square in the center that represented the cabin. Some of the figures were bunched together on the screen, and there appeared to be at least ten intruders.

"Unless grizzly bears travel in packs and plan strategy," McCarter commented, "I think the enemy has arrived."

Manning switched off the sonar and turned on the closed-circuit television. Surveillance cameras mounted in trees and equipped with infrared lenses were activated, and pale figures appeared on the screen. They marched through the dark, rifles and submachine guns clenched in their fists.

"Well," Manning announced. "It's official. We're surrounded by a bunch of guys who don't look like they want to sell us encyclopedias."

"Let's hit them before they hit us," Katz advised, grabbing his Uzi.

"I've got some toys that might help," Manning declared, heading for a grandfather clock in one corner of the room.

He inserted a key in the side and turned it and the clock popped open. Inside was a hidden weapons rack containing two FAL automatic rifles and a pair of M-79 grenade launchers, among other things. There were also two cases of ammo. Manning reached up to the top shelf and removed a shoulder-holster rig and a .357 Magnum Eagle pistol.

"You guys take the launchers," the Canadian instructed, sliding into the Horizontal Modular holster rig.

"I've got some other explosive surprises for our uninvited guests."

"Want to split up or stay together and play ring-around-a-rosy with these blokes?" McCarter asked, breaking open one of the grenade launchers. The M-79 resembled a sawed-off shotgun with a huge bore, but it took a 40mm cartridge-style grenade that made any buckshot load seem like a spitball.

"Stay together and cover one another," Katz replied. "And we'd better move before the invaders start kicking in the doors."

"Just a minute," Manning urged as he donned a back-pack. "I've got one more thing to do."

The Canadian yanked a throw rug from the floor and pried a loose board. He reached inside the gap and set the dial of a timing mechanism attached to a special detonator inserted in a pound and half of C-4 plastic explosives.

"Okay," Manning announced. "This whole place goes up in seven minutes. If we're not out of here by then, we'll go up with it."

"I hope the enemy doesn't get us pinned down for a minute or two," McCarter commented.

"Let's go out the back," Manning suggested. "The truck is out there and I want to head over to the toolshed to set up a reception for the night callers."

As the three Phoenix Force commandos plunged outside, the Russians positioned at the rear of the building opened fire. Bullets chewed chunks of wood from the cabin as the Phoenix fighters scrambled for the truck. The enemy was still more than two hundred yards away and Katz and McCarter, armed with short range subguns and the grenade launchers, held their fire.

Manning aimed a FAL rifle at the muzzle-flash of an opponent's weapon and squeezed off a quick 3-round burst. The shadowy form of a Russian gunman hopped backward as the copper-jacketed 7.62mm rounds plowed into his chest. The guy crashed to the earth and did not get up again.

Two Soviet triggermen fired at Manning, but the Canadian had already shifted to another position. Bullets rang against metal, richocheting off the steel frame of the truck. McCarter raised the stock of his M-79 to his shoulder and pointed it at the aggressors. The grenade launcher jarred his body as he fired the 40mm messenger of HE devastation. The missile sailed over the heads of the two Russian gunsels and exploded directly behind the pair, blasting both men into oblivion and hurling their mutilated bodies twelve feet.

Katz spotted more shapes advancing from the west side. He braced his grenade launcher against his hip and triggered a big 40mm problem solver. The grenade erupted in a ball of orange fury and the shredded corpse of a Russian invader shot up into the night sky as if from a trampoline. Two more Kremlin hitters kept coming. One man opened fire with a CAR-15 rifle and a stream of 5.56mm slugs sliced air above the Israeli's head as Katz hastily dropped to one knee.

The Phoenix Force unit commander discarded the empty M-79 and grabbed the Uzi that hung from a shoulder strap by his left side. Katz handled the Israeli chattergun as if he had been born with one attached to his hand. He fired a trio of 9mm rounds that chopped one opponent's chest into Russian goulash and hit the other gunman with a diagonal spray of parabellums. Bullets slashed a bloody line across the man's torso from left hip to right shoulder. His body collapsed across the still form of his comrade.

Manning dashed to the toolshed, firing a short burst from his FAL as he ran. He relied on his teammates to supply additional cover. Katz and McCarter did not disappoint their Canadian colleague. They fired twin volleys of 9mm rounds in the direction of the Russian hit team. A voice shrieked in pain, indicating that at least one bullet found human flesh.

"Pomagiteh!" a voice cried for help.

The Canadian warrior reached the toolshed and crouched beside the door. He quickly took a concave metal object from his backpack and set the curved Claymore mine by the corner of the shed, facing the house. Manning made certain the special radio-operated plunger of the Claymor's electrical squib was in place before he jogged back to the truck.

McCarter climbed into the truck and slid behind the wheel while Manning and Katz leaped into the pickup bed. A Soviet trooper charged forward and yanked the pin from an M-26 fragmentation grenade. Katz opened fire with his Uzi, tearing the guy open like a gutted deer. The Russian dropped his grenade and with both arms wrapped around his bullet-racked abdomen, the soldier glanced at his comrades. He realized they were close enough to be harmed by shrapnel from the frag grenade.

The man pitched his body over the M-26 just as the hand bomb exploded, blasting the Russian's body into a flying collage of blood, bones and chunks of meat. The other Soviet operatives gasped in horror as they watched their comrade burst apart like a balloon of water slammed against a sidewalk.

Katz had also witnessed the man's sacrifice to protect his fellow soldiers. The Phoenix Force commander admired the bravery of the Russian soldier. Katz was of Russian descent and he found no pleasure in shooting brave young Russians, but circumstances had made them the enemy.

Gary Manning removed a blue plastic disc from his pack. The object resembled a Frisbee and it was used in a similar manner. The Canadian demo expert turned the dial at the center of the disc and hurled it in a high, wide arc. The "Frisbee" whirled around the front of the cabin and descended toward the ground. Several Russians dashing toward the building stared at the flying saucer in astonishment.

Then the detonator ignited the battery-operated electrical squib and a quarter pound of C-4 exploded. Voices screamed into the night as the blast claimed two more Soviets. Their screams were barely a whisper amid the thunderous roar of the explosion.

McCarter stomped on the gas pedal and the Chevy pickup lunged forward. The Briton steered with his right hand as he held the Ingram machine pistol at the window with his left. The truck was a calculated risk. Their opponents were professionals who would know how to take out a vehicle. A well-placed grenade or a high velocity bullet through the windshield could stop them cold...cold dead. If even one Russian had a grenade or rocket launcher, he could simply stand back and pick off the truck with a single round.

But there was no alternative. If the Phoenix Force trio stayed put, they would be sitting targets for the Soviet hit team. Manning had already created a seven minute deadline before they left the cabin. They had less than four minutes remaining before the log house would erupt in a violent flash.

Dimitri Lagunin raised his Remington rifle and aimed at the windshield of the truck. The cross hairs found McCarter's face, marking his forehead. Lagunin began to squeeze the trigger, but McCarter was driving in an irregular zigzag pattern, trying to prevent giving the enemy an easy target.

The Remington rasped as a .308 projectile rocketed from the sound suppressor. The big bullet smashed a hole through the reinforced glass of the windshield. The slug missed McCarter by less than six inches and burrowed into the backrest. McCarter flinched as one might if a bird unexpectedly flew past one's face.

"Bleedin' bastard," McCarter rasped, searching the area for the sniper.

Lagunin once again worked the bolt action of his Remington. McCarter saw the long barrel with the silencer extension, he saw the outline of the Morkrie Dela gunman as Lagunin started to aim his weapon once more. The Briton steered the truck toward the Russian and shoved his boot on the gas.

The Chevy pickup charged straight for the startled KGB assassin. Lagunin's hands shook as he tried to aim the rifle and he realized that even if he killed the driver, the truck might still run him down. Lagunin's nerve broke. He wanted to survive more than he wanted to stop the men in the truck.

He leaped away from the path of the speeding vehicle and hit the ground in a tumbling roll.

McCarter extended his left arm through the window on the driver's side. Firing "weak hand" from a moving vehicle, the Briton could not manage any sort of accuracy and compensated by spraying the area with a long burst of 9mm rounds. Lagunin's body twitched and bounced against the ground as half-a-dozen parabellum slugs smashed his form into a slab of lifeless meat, dripping crimson from numerous wounds.

"Silly sod," McCarter muttered the brief epitaph and continued to drive from the cabin.

At least two Russian combatants at the rear of the cabin opened fire. The flames of their automatic rifles sliced through the darkness and high-velocity projectiles sang sourly against the frame of the fleeing pickup. One bullet split the metal skin of the vehicle within inches of Manning's left elbow.

"Shit," the Canadian rasped, taking a small radio transceiver no larger than a pocket calculator from his pocket.

He pressed a button, transmitting an ultrahigh-frequency signal to the radio detonator hooked up to the Claymore mine he had planted at the toolshed. The Claymore exploded, sending out a monstrous concussion wave and razor-edged shrapnel. The blast blew apart an entire shed wall. The roof collapsed and slid forward to crash down on the Russian gunmen, and their bodies were crushed into bloodied pulp.

Sergeant Viilov staggered across the grounds, blood oozing from a deep gash in his thigh. The Russian noncom had been hit by a shard of flying shrapnel, but he was still on his feet. Apparently he was the only survivor of the Soviet hit team. Viilov placed the buttstock of his M-16 to a shoulder and tried to train it on the fleeing vehicle.

Then the world seemed to erupt in a ball of white fire.

Seven minutes had passed. The bomb Manning had activated under the floorboards of the cabin exploded.

Viilov's head was literally blasted from his shoulders and his body was ripped apart.

As the truck continued to speed away from the battle site, Manning said, "Well, we made it."

"Yes," Katz said grimly. "But this is just round one, Gary. I have a feeling the main event won't be this easy."

"You thought that was easy, Yakov?" the Canadian asked.

"No," Katz replied. "That's my point."

8

Manning, McCarter and Katz were forced to abandon the Chevy. The truck was riddled with bullet holes and would have certainly drawn unwanted attention. Besides, the KGB obviously knew a great deal about Manning. They must have known about the Canadian's cabin and recognized his Jeep Cherokee. That meant they would probably know about the pickup, too.

They ditched the vehicle near Meadow Lake. Reluctantly, the trio disassembled all their weapons except the pistols. Manning had a duffel bag and an extra backpack in the truck and the FAL, grenade launchers and Katz's Uzi went into the bag. McCarter insisted on carrying his disassembled Ingram machine pistol in a pack strapped to his back. The trio continued to move south on foot. At a public telephone booth, they finally called Stony Man.

"Grayland Insurance Agency," the pleasant voice of a young woman announced cheerfully. "Our office is closed for business at this time, but we hope to reopen operations in two months. If you have a message for any of our officers, please leave your name and telephone number at the sound of the tone, and thank you for calling Grayland Agencies."

Katz heard the dull beep and spoke into the mouthpiece of the receiver. "This is Conrad Goldberg, with S and O Enterprises."

He read the number of the public phone into the receiver and hung up. S and O was a simple code that could be broken by anyone with a push-button telephone in the States.

The letters were on the numbered buttons while "and" referred to the number one. This same code had been used by advertisers for years and Katz had used it to give the area code of the phone number that would otherwise have betrayed their location in Canada to any unwanted ears listening on a wire tap.

The phone rang less than a minute later. Katz answered it and a familiar voice said, "Mr. Goldberg? This is Whceler."

"Hello, Mr. Wheeler." Katz smiled. The voice belonged to Aaron Kurtzman, the computer expert at Stony Man operations. The headquarters had been attacked by enemy forces more than a year ago and Kurtzman had been shot in the spine. The rugged bearded computer jockey, affectionately known as "the Bear," was crippled for life and confined to a wheelchair. "Wheeler" was Kurtzman's dark-humored joke.

"Didn't expect to hear from you, Goldberg," the Bear declared. "Has something gone wrong with your vacation plans?"

"Drastically wrong," Katz answered. "Our equipment broke down and even the car died on the freeway. Then, believe it or not, a plane crashed into our summer house and destroyed it."

"Holy shit," Kurtzman replied. He realized the Phoenix Force commander would not give exact details on the telephone regardless of whether it was a secure line or not, but Katz had still described disaster. The three Phoenix fighters in Canada had been attacked. They were on foot, low on ammunition and the cabin they had been at was either destroyed or unsafe. "I hope no one was hurt?"

"None of the family even got a scratch," Katz assured him, letting the Bear know that none of Phoenix Force had been injured. "However, the pilot and passengers were killed."

"That's awful," the Bear said, aware that Katz had just told him that they had killed some of the assailants.

"If I was paranoid I'd think it was some sort of plot by the KGB to ruin our vacation," Katz said with a laugh.

Kurtzman's fist tightened around the handset of the international transceiver in the control center of Stony Man headquarters. The Israeli was not joking and that meant Phoenix Force was facing the worst kind of danger.

"We're going to Michael Saunders's house at 6868 Crest Street," Katz stated. "Could you contact our sales personnel to meet us there? Try to get some of this mess ironed out."

"Of course," Kurtzman assured him. "We'll get on it right away."

"Thank you," Katz replied. "I hope everything is going all right at the home office."

"As far as I know," the Bear said, a cold shiver traveling up his damaged spine. The Israeli was warning him that Stony Man itself may be a target of the KGB.

"Well, keep in touch," Katz said. "I've got to go."

"Jesus," Kurtzman muttered as he switched off transmission and hastily wheeled his chair to the keyboard of the main computer.

He punched in the name Michael Saunders and hit the Search button. Data appeared on the monitor. Michael Saunders was one of Gary Manning's cover names. The three Phoenix Force members were heading for another piece of property owned by the Canadian warrior. If the cabin in Canada had been attacked, that meant Manning's cover was burned already. They had to have a good reason for heading to another site owned by Manning.

Kurtzman punched in the numbers 6868. The computer flashed "Insufficient Data." The Bear considered the push-button phone code. Six is MNO and eight is TUV. These letters could mean a great many things. The Bear was probably looking for an abbreviation. NV could be Nevada, but Manning did not own any property in that state...at least, not according to the computer. An abbreviation for Ontario might be OT. Manning had an apartment there, but it was too obvious. The KGB certainly knew about it.

"MT," Kurtzman mused, punching the keyboard buttons. "What have we got?"

The monitor offered a number of choices, including Mountain Time, Metric Ton, Montana, Machine Translation, Matthew, Mount, Mountain, Machine Technician and Mediterranean Theater of Operations.

Kurtzman cleared the screen; 6868 indicated MTMT, he decided. Or perhaps, MTmt. He fed it into the computer to confirm what he already suspected. The Bear smiled when the answer agreed with his assumption.

"Montana mountains," Kurtzman read the computer deduction aloud. "Manning must have some property in Montana he didn't bother to tell us about. Figures these guys would keep some secrets from us. What the hell, we keep stuff secret from them, too. I just hope Manning didn't keep this a secret from the rest of Phoenix Force."

"What's up, Aaron?" Hal Brognola asked as he entered the control center. A glance at the troubled expression on the Bear's face was all the Fed had to see to know something was very wrong.

"Maybe the beginning of the end," Kurtzman replied as he wheeled himself away from the computer panel.

KATZ, MANNING AND MCCARTER surreptitiously crossed the border into the United States. Manning had withdrawn a bundle of cash from one of his bank accounts registered under a phony name. He had superbly detailed documentation to pass security checks, and had kept his false ID secret from Stony Man. The headquarters had been attacked and raided once, and it could happen again. If it did and Manning's other ID and covers were burned, he wanted to be sure he had something to fall back on.

This was the reason he had not given Stony Man any information about his Montana property until now. The best way to keep a secret is not to tell anyone about it. He trusted Brognola, but he did not trust certain elements of the government of the United States. He was also concerned about the ability of Stony Man to maintain security. The raid on the headquarters proved that no security is airtight.

Despite all Manning's precautions, however, his cover had been burned. They would try to find out later what had gone wrong, but for now Phoenix had to concentrate on the clear and present danger of the KGB.

Katz and McCarter were surprised to discover Manning's property in Montana was another cabin site almost identical to the one in Saskatchewan. Getting to the cabin had been tough. Although they bought a Jeep from a used-car lot in Govenick, the vehicle could not climb the rock walls to Manning's hideaway. They had to scale the mountain by hand and footholds, and all three men were exhausted by the time they reached their destination.

"Beautiful up here, isn't it?" Manning asked his partners. "It's all mountain range around here. The closest town is about sixty miles away. The closest city is almost a hundred. It's at the rim of Glacier National Park."

"How did you manage to build anything up here?" Katz asked, impressed by what Manning had accomplished.

"An American business associate owned a construction company in Seattle," the Canadian explained. "He needed some demolition work done to clear land for a fifteen-million-dollar housing project. I agreed to handle the job and in return he flew out a team of workers and building materials to this mountain. Stuff had to be delivered by helicopter. All of this was done on the QT and there was no paperwork involved. I didn't even want Stony Man to know about this place, but I guess there's no choice now."

McCarter gazed across the rows of mountain peaks set against the crystal-blue skies. "You told us about it. Gave me the details to fly here in a chopper. Too bad we couldn't get one."

"Maybe we can get one from Brognola," Katz commented. "Did you share the directions to this place with Rafael and Calvin?"

"With Rafael and Keio," Manning answered. "I trust Calvin, but I just never got around to telling him about it. If he and Rafael are okay they should be able to get here sooner or later."

The Canadian fell silent when the sound of whirling blades cutting air drifted in with the wind. A dot appeared in the distance, a speck against the sky, approaching rapidly. The aircraft was a helicopter, but they didn't know if it was friend or foe. All three men headed for cover, grabbing weapons instinctively. The chopper kept coming and gradually descended to a wide, flat summit on the mountain.

When the wirlybird landed, sliding doors opened and three familiar figures emerged as Calvin James, Rafael Encizo and Hal Brognola climbed out the Huey. The other three members of Phoenix Force were relieved to see their partners had arrived safe and sound.

"You fellas move fast," Brognola remarked, shaking hands with Manning. "Figured we'd get here before you guys could get out of Canada."

"We didn't think we should waste any time, Hal," Katz replied. "Good to see you two," he told James and Encizo. "We were afraid you might have encountered the same trouble we found in Canada."

"No," Encizo answered. "We were just swimming around in Lake Michigan. Nobody was hunting us, not even confused sharks."

"At least nobody we know of," James added.

"Fill us in on the details," Brognola ordered. "All I know is we've got one hell of a mess that might be bad enough to force us to close shop, at least for a while."

Manning, McCarter and Katz told the story in detail while Encizo and James grimly listened to the tale. Brognola chewed the butt of a cigar that had gone out. He did not relight the stogie until they finished the story.

"Yakov," the Fed began, "you've been involved in this international intrigue business longer than any of us. How do you evaluate this situation?"

"I suspect the KGB has a general idea about Phoenix Force," Katz began, fishing a pack of Camels from his pocket. "The security leak might be with Stony Man, but I suspect it came from another source, maybe CIA records or the old Royal Canadian Mounted Police intel files. God knows how those were treated after the SIS took over that department. Or it could be a leak with the BND or CSG-9 in Germany.''

"But the Russians have associated Manning with Phoenix or at least with something like Phoenix," Brognola mused.

"I've been wondering about that," Katz said. "And I think I know how that happened. Check with the Greek authorities. I bet they made a deal with the Soviets and sent Colonel Kostov back to the iron curtain."

"He was the Bulgarian operating on Krio Island, right?" Brognola asked.

"And he got a good look at all of us except David, who was recovering from a flesh wound at the time," Katz answered. "Now, Rafael, David and Cal have never been officially connected with an intel organization unless one includes Phoenix Force and Stony Man. However, Gary and I have been members of intel outfits before. The Kremlin probably has files on both of us. They simply went after Gary first."

"So Stony Man isn't a target," Manning assured Brognola. "At least, we don't think it is...yet."

"The KGB tried to take Gary alive," Katz explained. "That means they wanted information. If they manage to capture any one of us alive, they may be able to use drugs or torture to get us to talk. Nobody can remain silent forever if the KGB works on them hard enough."

"You're sure it's the KGB?" the Fed asked. "You've got a lot of enemies out there. MERGE or TRIO might be responsible."

"The hit wasn't their style," Katz insisted. "And both Gary and I overheard opponents speaking Russian. I don't think there's any doubt who we're up against, Hal."

"So how do we handle it?" Brognola asked. "Like you said, Yakov, if they catch one of you guys it could ruin Stony Man."

"If they catch us alive," McCarter stated. "We'll just have to be certain that doesn't happen."

"There are two choices of action," Katz declared. "One is to disband Phoenix Force for a while. To be safe, you'd have to get rid of Gary and me. We'd have to leave the country for a year or more. Probably couldn't return until we'd gotten new identities and probably some cosmetic surgery done."

"I hope I like your other idea better." Brognola frowned.

"The other choice is to let us take the offense," Katz answered. "The Soviets are hunting us, but with a bit of luck, maybe we can get them first."

"I'm sure that idea appeals to you guys," the Fed replied. "But what good will it do? How are you going to find them? And even if you do the Kremlin will just send more agents in the future."

"Not in the near future," Katz answered. "Not if what I suspect is true."

"What's that, Yakov?" Brognola asked.

"You see," McCarter said, "we've been doing a bit of thinking about that hit on the cabin site. Those blokes wern't just KGB. They were bleedin' commandos and they would have chopped us to pieces if Gary hadn't installed sophisticated security devices and had a lot of explosive surprises up his sleeve."

"We believe," Katz began, "that the Soviets have sent a special unit comprised of both KGB and Russian commandos to hunt us down and destroy us. If that's true, we've probably encountered just a small portion of the attack force. If we can find the others and hit them first, the price will be too great for the Soviets to want to take that sort of risk again. Perhaps they'll try again in the future, but not until they believe they have a better plan for wiping us out entirely."

"You're sure about that?" Brognola asked.

"I can't make any promises one way or the other," the Israeli admitted. "But Moscow is practical. They won't indulge in revenge if it gets too expensive."

"You're talking about one hell of a risk," the Fed remarked. "If anything goes wrong, we'll all be sunk."

"Hal," Encizo began, "we've all been taking big risks for a long time. Let us take this one."

"Okay," Brognola said with a shrug. "How do we begin?"

"Soviet agents are usually brought into this country directly through the Soviet embassies and the United Nations. Try to find out about any new faces among the Russian delegates. The National Security Agency keeps tabs on that sort of thing...at least they try to."

"Yeah." Brognola nodded. "Then we'll find out what we have on the sons of bitches. What else can we do at my end?"

"We'll need more equipment," Katz explained. "And we'll need to have transportation available to travel anywhere in the United States or Canada at a moment's notice. When that happens we'll probably need connections with intel sources in whatever area we land. CIA, NSA, FBI or whoever has the most manpower and influence."

"Okay," Brognola agreed. "We'll do what we can, but this is a different situation than you fellas have had to handle in the past."

"The basics remain the same, Hal," Katz told him. "Kill or be killed."

9

"Do you know what they would say in English about your performance, Captain Shatrov?" Major Potapov began as he poured some vodka into a glass. "You really fucked up."

Boris Shatrov sat stiffly in a straight-backed chair in a hotel suite in the heart of New York City. Lieutenant Colonel Vladimir Burov, his aide Captain Myshko and Potapov had met with Shatrov when the Morkrie Dela agent arrived from Canada to report his failure. Shatrov looked at Burov, hoping the KGB colonel would come to his defense. Burov was clearly annoyed by Potapov's remark, but he did not argue with the GRU officer.

"There was nothing wrong with how we carried out the attempt to abduct and later kill the Canadian," Shatrov declared, forced to make his own defense. "I am a professional, Major Potapov. I have carried out many liquidations for the state in the past. There was nothing wrong with how we handled this assignment."

"Then why is Gary Manning still alive?" the GRU officer asked. "He was too clever for you, Comrade. You tried to 'cowboy' the assignment, as the American intelligence would say. You rushed into it without proper planning. You should have known better. This man and his teammates are professionals and that is why they slipped through your fingers. Not once, Comrade, but twice."

"My orders were to capture Manning alive for interrogation," Shatrov stated. "Failing this, I was to kill him. If I could have simply killed the man, he would be dead now."

"Because you failed to kidnap him and failed to kill him *twice*," Potapov scoffed. "You should go back to arranging accidents for dissidents, Comrade. You're certainly no match for men such as Manning."

"That's enough, Major," Colonel Burov said sharply. "The Canadian gangster got away and that is all that matters. Giving Captain Shatrov a tongue-lashing won't change anything."

"Isn't it fortunate Major Shalnev is not present?" Potapov remarked. "He might be tempted to lash out with more than his tongue. Thanks to Shatrov's carelessness, ten paratroopers were killed."

"And so were eight of my men," Shatrov snapped. He immediately regretted the statement because it merely reminded the others of the number of Soviet operatives slain under his command.

"Eighteen of our people are dead." Potapov shook his head. "But Comrade Shatrov didn't get a scratch."

"A commander doesn't have to go to the front lines to do his job, Major," Burov stated. "His duty is to coordinate the battle and strategy. Comrade Shatrov acted accordingly."

"And failed, Comrade Colonel," Potapov said with a shrug.

"Major," Burov began, "do I have to remind you who has been placed in charge of this mission?"

"I know you're in charge, Colonel," Potapov said, sighing. "But that doesn't mean I have to remain silent when brave Russian soldiers get killed because one of your men is careless and overeager."

"One of *my* men, Major," Burov stated. "That means his reprimand and discipline, if any, are my responsibility. Not yours, Major. You are not KGB."

"Thank God for that," Potapov commented, gulping down his vodka.

"What does that mean?" Burov demanded.

"Oh, God is a concept of a supreme being that is not recognized by the Soviet government or the Communist party,"

Potapov answered. "Of course, I used this expression in jest."

"Your jest is not amusing, Major," Burov warned.

"I don't think it is amusing when Russian soldiers are killed, either, Comráde Burov," Potapov told him, heading for the vodka bottle. "You KGB don't have much use for the Russian army, but GRU is basically concerned with military intelligence. I don't like Russian soldiers getting killed because an ass like Shatrov smelled blood and rushed in for the kill. One difference between your organization and mine, Colonel, is that GRU doesn't have Morkrie Dela department. We believe homicidal maniacs should be locked up in jails along with such dangerous enemies of the state as subversives who sell old jazz records and Levi's jeans to the Soviet people...."

"Damn it!" Burov snapped. "If you were not a war hero with a Gold Star I would think you a traitor, Potapov!"

"I am no traitor, Comrade," Potapov told him. "I am proud to be a Russian, but that doesn't mean I have to like everything the Soviet government does...or the KGB."

"You can like or dislike whatever you choose, Comrade," Burov said tensely. "But you'd better learn to keep your mouth shut, Major."

"Excuse me for interrupting," Captain Myshko began. "But may I suggest we concentrate on our mission? The Canadian, Manning, has escaped. What shall we do next? Find the man with one hand or try to locate the Canadian?"

"Perhaps both," Burov answered. "Major Shalnev and a detachment of his troops are going to meet us in Georgia. Then we are going to pay a visit on Heinz Muller."

"But we don't know that the German is involved with the enemy commandos," Potapov said. "It might be the Israeli, Katzenelenbogen, or perhaps someone we don't have on file. After all, there is nothing in the records about the other three men we seek."

"The German is an enemy of the Soviet Union and the revolution of the working people throughout the world," Burov said with a shrug. "So who cares if he dies?"

"That's brilliant logic, Comrade," Potapov muttered. "Why don't we assassinate the American President while we're here, too?"

"Is that supposed to be a joke, Major?" Burov glared at him.

"Nyet, Tovarisch." Potapov assured him. "I guess I'm just daydreaming outloud."

HEINZ MULLER had come a long way since he was a private in the German army during World War II. One of the earliest recruits into Hitler's Youth Corps, Muller had lied about his age in order to enlist and serve the fatherland. He was only fifteen when he served under Rommel in Africa. However, the enthusiastic youth soon earned a promotion to sergeant and eventually received the Iron Cross for valor.

Yet Muller had become disillusioned with the Nazi party and did not join it when he became an adult. Of course, by then the war over Germany had fallen in defeat. Muller returned to Africa and eventually wound up with the security forces in the Sudan. He became a professional mercenary and served in numerous campaigns. His main opposition to communism had little to do with politics. The capitalists paid better and they were less apt to use mercs for cannon fodder. Muller's politics were very simple. He believed in himself and doing what was in his own best interests.

Although Muller's patriotism may have been questionable, his results were generally quite impressive. He was a good strategist and courageous in battle. His inflated ego made him deaf to advice that occasionally cost him a battle, but he won more than he lost and he usually managed to blame defeat on someone else.

At the age of fifty-five, Muller was heavyset and thick around the waist. He dyed his hair with a blue-black tint, and the dye tended to streak on his scrub-brush mustache, allowing patches of gray to poke through. Muller wore a variety of prosthetics attached to the stump at his right wrist. His favorite device was a knife with an eight-inch, double-edged blade. It had limited use except for close-quarter combat, but it made a hell of an impression on the men.

Muller's men were survivalists, individuals who believed they would need combat and survival skills to cope with a national or international disaster in the near future. These survivalists were concerned about nuclear war, economic turmoil, worldwide famine and other horrendous ordeals.

Muller taught a two-month course in survivalist training at his camp a few miles west of the Savannah River. His students were mostly sincere, eager men between the ages eighteen and forty-five, and his course was similar to the basic training offered in any branch of the armed forces, except that there was little time spent on drill and cere- mony. Most of the training concerned firearms. Muller rambled on and on about guns. His lectures made him sound more like an arms dealer trying to peddle his prod- ucts than a survivalist instructor. However, most of his clients sat spellbound when he discussed staggered-row box magazines, barley-corn sights and steel trunnion blocks. Most of them had no idea what the hell he was talking about, but they were certainly impressed.

The staff at the camp were former mercenaries who were no longer able to make a living in the soldier-of-fortune business. They had discovered the hard way that the lure of big adventure for big dollars was usually an empty dream. They had found themselves in stinking jungles, often poorly armed and half-starved. Many of their employers ripped them off and mercs were often used as cannon fodder or assigned to high-risk missions that regular troops would not accept. The money was never as much as they expected and it certainly did not equal the risks involved.

Working as instructors at Muller's survivalist camp was a hell of a lot safer. The pay was reasonable and the ex- mercs were treated as heroes by the trainees. Most of the younger volunteers hoped to become mercenaries after they graduated. Let them find out the hard way, too. It was the only way most guys would ever learn.

"I should have stayed in the Corps, man," Dan Calden remarked to Josh Rook as the two mercs drove roving patrol around the fifty square acres of the training camp. "If I had just stayed in, I'd be about ready to retire now with a twenty year pension from the Marines."

"They never would have kept you in the Corps, Calden," Rook said with a chuckle. "Ain't you heard? The Marines are looking for a few *good* men."

"Up yours, Rook," Calden muttered as he steered the old rebuilt Army Jeep along the fenced perimeter of the camp. "I mean it, man. This fuckin' place is getting to me. Running these dip-shit 'cruits through a crash course in mayhem and sending them outta here thinking they know how to take care of themselves if a nuclear war breaks out. It's bullshit."

"Who cares?" Rook said with a shrug. "Nobody twists their arms to come here. If they pick up some self-confidence, that's more than they had when they first showed up. Just pick up your paycheck and be happy you ain't washing dishes, jarhead."

"This roving patrol is bullshit, too," Calden complained. "What the hell are we supposed to be guarding this place from? Does Muller figure the Girl Scouts are gonna launch a panty raid on the camp?"

"Wishful thinking." Rook laughed. "But Muller would never allow any of us to do any humping on post, even with grown-up girls. That's against his lofty moral standards."

"Yeah," Calden muttered. "Where's Muller get off makin' us march to church every Sunday?"

"Maybe he's a born-again Christian," Rook suggested.

"Then he should be handing out booklets on street corners," Calden growled. "Or become a missionary and go convert the cannibals in the Congo or something. He shouldn't be running a camp for killers."

"Didn't you ever hear of Christian soldiers?" Rook said, grinning. "Look, Calden. This is all part of the show. Muller isn't off the track with this survivalist place. He's making money and looking like a saint in the process. No-body gets hurt, so big deal.''

"So it's okay for him to take and take from these poor slobs?" Calden shook his head with dismay. "And to think that they call us mercenaries."

The Jeep continued to creep through the camp at a slow pace, allowing the pair to observe the area under the beams of the Jeep's headlights. The camp was quiet at night. A couple of trainees were on guard duty beside the fence, but most were sound asleep in their bunks.

"Halt and be recognized!" the voice of a trainee sentry cried out.

"Oh, shit," Rook muttered. "Dumb ass probably spotted a goddamn deer...."

The rasping cough of a silenced weapon uttered three rapid reports. The sentry, stationed at the side of the fence, hopped backward and fell on his back, a trio of ragged bullet holes forming a crooked line across his fatigue shirt.

"Christ!" Calden exclaimed, fumbling for the pump shotgun in the back of the Jeep.

"What the hell—" Rook began.

The windshield erupted and glass shattered as bullets smashed through the pane and chopped into Josh Rook's torso. He convulsed in agony and cried out as blood poured from holes in his camouflage bush jacket. The mercenary slumped against the dashboard, muscles twitching slightly as death claimed Rook for his final enlistment.

Dan Calden jumped out of the Jeep and pumped the action of his shotgun, jacking a shell into the chamber. Another volley of bullets from the sound suppressor of a full-auto weapon slammed into the second merc. The impact spun him around to receive three more slugs in the spine and right kidney. Calden triggered his Winchester pump, blasting a load of buckshot into the night sky. It was the final futile gesture of his young life.

The shotgun blast alerted others inside the camp. Trainees emerged from the barracks, more curious than frightened. The mercenaries who stumbled from the NCO quarters assumed the shots had been fired by an overeager sentry or a drunken instructor. None of them came outside with a weapon in hand.

"Sweet Jesus!" a trainee gasped when he saw half a dozen figures in black night-camouflage uniforms and matching berets charge across the grounds.

The assault force carried a variety of weapons. Most were armed with American-made firearms: M-16 assault rifles stolen from military arms rooms to be sold on the black market and M-76 submachine guns hijacked en route from the Smith & Wesson factory to delivery at police departments in Boston. Some other weapons had been acquired through similar illegal means and converted to fire full-auto. Many of the gunmen were armed with Soviet AK-74 assault rifles and PPS submachine guns.

The trainees were surprised, but not many were truly frightened. They assumed this was probably a training exercise to test their ability to cope with an unexpected night assault. Others realized the purpose of this exercise did not make sense since none of the trainees was allowed to keep weapons in their billets. The merc instructors knew it was not a test. Most ran back inside the NCO quarters to arm themselves while one merc ran forward to shout a warning at the trainees.

The invaders opened fire. A stream of 7.62mm rounds ripped into the lone merc. The guy's body hurtled six feet backward and hit the ground in a tumbling roll. Other aggressors fired salvos of full-auto death into the trainees outside the billets. The hapless victims were plastered against the wall of the building, blood spilling from butchered flesh.

A window shattered as a merc smashed glass with the barrel of a CAR 15. He fired back at the invaders. A Russian commando screamed as two 5.56mm projectiles burned into his chest. The Soviet soldier collapsed as several others countered with full-auto bursts that smashed the remaining portion of windowpane and splintered the surrounding frame. The merc fell back and landed on the floor, his face shattered by high-velocity bullets.

"Fucking bastards!" Hank Nichols snarled as he crawled away from his slain comrade to a footlocker at the end of his bed.

Nichols unlocked the case and threw open the lid to get his hands on some special weaponry. The merc removed an Argentine 9mm PA3-DM submachine gun. The compact subgun resembled a cross between an Israeli Uzi and old American M-3 greasegun. Nichols inserted an extended magazine, chambered a round and gathered two M-26 frag grenades from his locker.

"You guys want a fight," the merc rasped, "I'll give you a fuckin' fight, man!"

Another survivalist instructor hit the floor, most of his skull blown away from three AK rounds in the forehead. The guy fell near Nichols's feet, brains pouring from his shattered cranium. Nichols jumped over the dead man and scrambled to a window.

He lobbed a grenade through the broken pane and hurried to another position. Nichols heard the M-26 explode, and voices shrieked in agony. The merc nodded in grim satisfaction and appeared at another window. Two Russian commandos stared back at the survivalist pro as Nichols squeezed the trigger. A volley of parabellum slugs slammed into the Soviet hitmen, punching through chests and faces. The pair dropped dead before either man could fire a shot.

"How do you assholes like that, man!" Nichols shouted, yanking the pin from another grenade.

"*Grana'ta!*" Major Shalnev, the commander of the Soviet paratroopers shouted. "Fire!"

A pair of Russians had set up an AG-17 automatic grenade launcher. The fearsome weapon mounted on a tripod fired three 30mm projectiles at the NCO quarters. The billets was ripped apart by the high-explosive charges that blasted the place into kindling. The grenade team altered the aim of the AG-17 and opened fire on the trainee billets, blowing the building to bits and killing the remaining unarmed men inside.

"Who are these invaders?" Heinz Muller cried in rage as he charged from his bedroom to the office at the headquarters building. "How dare the devils attack my domain!"

Muller wore his double-edged prosthesis at the end of his right arm and carried a .45-calibar General Officer pistol in his left fist. Information about the pistol flashed through his mind.

Semiautomatic, recoil operated with a blade front sight and square notch back sight, he thought. Muzzle velocity, 210 meters per second....

This was Muller's way of countering fear in combat. He tried to convince himself that the pistol would make him more than a match for anything he had to handle. He was Heinz Muller, veteran of a hundred campaigns, winner of the Iron Cross. These *Schwienehunden* did not know who they were fucking with. He would show them the price they would pay in blood!

The door burst open and a Russian tumbled across the threshold in a fast shoulder roll. Muller aimed his pistol at the doorway, aware another Soviet attacker would cover the first man inside the office. A Russian peered around the corner, a PPS machine gun in his fists. Muller's pistol roared, blasting a 230-grain slug through the soldier's face. The big bullet split the bridge of his nose, tunneled through brain matter and smashed open the back of his skull.

"*Scheisser!*" Muller snarled as he turned toward the Russian who had rolled across the floor.

The soldier raised an M-76 subgun and tried to aim it at Muller, but the German merc fired his .45 autoloader and a solid ball projectile smashed into the Russian's head just below the hairline. The top of his skull popped off like a lid, splattering brains against the nearest wall.

A third Soviet commando charged into the office. Muller pivoted to confront the newest opponent as the Russian swung a butt stroke with the hard plastic stock of his M-16 rifle. The German grunted when the rifle butt stamped his left forearm, jarring the .45 pistol from his grasp.

The Russian slashed the barrel of his M-16 at Muller's face, but the veteran survivalist ducked under the attack and thrust his right arm forward. The Soviet hitman screamed as sharp steel pierced his solar plexus. Blood spewed across Muller's wrist. He shoved hard, driving the point of his knife upward to puncture the Russian's heart.

"I'll kill you all!" Muller declared as he spat in the soldier's face and yanked the blade from the dying man's chest.

Suddenly a fist rocketed into Muller's face. The punch smashed the merc's nose, breaking the bridge. Blood oozed from his nostrils as he staggered backward. Major Shalnev stepped into the office, a PPS subgun in his left hand. He grabbed the pistol grip of the Soviet chatterbox and aimed the weapon at Muller.

"Surrender," Shalnev ordered in thickly accented English.

"Donnerwetter!" Muller replied, suddenly lunging for a CAR-15 in a rifle rack near his desk.

Shalnev fired a quick salvo. Bullets smashed into the rifle rack and wall, spitting plaster dust into Muller's face. The German leaped back from the wall and fell against the corner of the desk. Shalnev moved closer as Muller wiped his eyes with his single hand.

"Surrender," Shalnev repeated. "I will not tell you—"

Muller suddenly grabbed the edge of the desk to brace himself and lashed a roundhouse kick to the major's PPS. His boot struck the subgun from Shalnev's hands. Muller slashed a cross-body stroke with the knife at the end of his right arm. The Russian hissed with pain as the sharp steel sliced open his black tunic and cut flesh on his chest.

The German merc lunged with the point of his knife, but Shalnev sidestepped the attack and hooked the heel of his left palm into Muller's wrist to deflect the knife thrust. The Russian officer whirled, stepping behind his opponent. Shalnev's right hand lashed a karate chop to Muller's right kidney. He followed through with an elbow smash between the German's shoulder blades.

Muller groaned, stumbled forward and suddenly pivoted, slashing with his bladed hand once more. Shalnev weaved out of range and quickly launched a powerful straight kick. The heel of his boot slammed under Muller's jaw with fearsome force. The merc's head snapped back with such might, vertebrae cracked. Heinz Muller fell backward, his head striking the corner of the desk. The back of his skull cracked open on impact and he fell lifeless to the floor.

"Major Shalnev," Leonid Potapov called as he appeared at the doorway. "Good God! This room looks like a miniature battlefield!"

"Da." Shalnev confirmed, glancing down at Muller's corpse. "The German died bravely. Unfortunately, he killed three of my men. This mission sickens me, Major Potapov, and I don't give a damn if they know how I feel in Moscow."

"Careless remarks can cost you dearly, my friend," Potapov warned. "I know from experience. Don't let our comrades from the KGB hear you speak in such a manner."

"Damn them, too," Shalnev spat. "I did not see them in battle. My men took the risks. My men were forced to commit this slaughter for the Kremlin. Most of the Americans were not even armed. I am a fighting man, Major. I was not trained to make war on unarmed civilians."

"This was supposed to be a paramilitary base," Potapov said with a shrug. "We could not afford to take any chances."

"The KGB did not take any chances, Major," Shalnev said angrily. "But several of my men are dead!"

"Is there a problem, Comrade Shalnev?" Colonel Burov inquired as he stepped across the threshold.

"I am not a Communist, Colonel," Shalnev replied. "Please do not call me 'comrade.'"

"You're a Russian soldier," Burov snapped. "That makes us comrades to a common cause whether you like it or not." He stared down at Muller. "We wanted that one alive."

"I tried to take him alive, Colonel," Shalnev explained. "But he forced me to kill him. Check his body. You will find no bullet holes. I killed him with my hands and feet."

"How very impressive." Burov smiled. "Well, search this camp for any evidence linking Muller with Manning or any of the other commandos we seek. Then we'll burn the place to the ground and continue our mission."

10

Dashiell McQueen's parents were mystery-novel readers, which explained his unlikely first name. Perhaps this also had something to do with how McQueen became a member of the National Security Agency. Most Americans know little or nothing about the NSA, yet it is actually much larger and more widespread than either the CIA or the FBI.

Sidney Nazarov was a case officer for the Central Intelligence Agency. An American born of Russian defectors who fled to the United States during the reign of Stalin, Nazarov was raised speaking both English and Russian. He was violently opposed to Communism of any kind. Nazarov hated Commies with a passion, but second on his list of the most loathsome forms of human life was the NSA.

The two agents exchanged dagger stares as they sat at the small conference table in a rented meeting room of the Pleasant House Motel on the outskirts of Watford City, North Dakota. McQueen and Nazarov would never have been forced to work together unless extraordinary circumstances required their special expertise. McQueen had been involved in NSA surveillance of Soviet personnel at the United Nations for more than five years, and Nazarov had formerly operated as a mole within the Soviet Union itself.

The five men of Phoenix Force needed these two unique espionage pros, and they did not give a damn if McQueen and Nazarov hated each other's guts. Intelligence networks seldom get along and resentment among them is common. The NSA tends to feel that the CIA and FBI gets credit for successes that the National Security Agency participated in, as well. The CIA, on the other hand, also catches hell for activities carried out by the lesser-known NSA.

The other members of Phoenix Force looked to Yakov Katzenelenbogen to preside over the meeting. Stony Man operations had managed to get them the best support CIA and NSA had to offer, but it would be up to Katz to get everyone to work together on a mission that only Phoenix knew all the details of.

"Mr. McQueen," the Israeli began, "will you present the information concerning KGB operatives known to have recently entered the country via the United Nations Soviet delegation?"

"The most interesting new arrival is Vladimir Georgevich Booruv...." the NSA agent began, reading from a report.

"Burov," Nazarov corrected. "It is pronounced *Burov*, Mr. McQueen."

"Is this an intelligence operation or a course in Russian?" McQueen said sharply. "Anyway, Burov is a lieutenant colonel in the KGB. In 1979 he was expelled from Great Britain for espionage. We can only guess how long he was operating in London as a double agent."

"If he was a member of the British SIS then you know how long he was operating there, don't you?" Nazarov sneered.

"Burov was using the alias Wilford Jessup when he was recruited into British intelligence," McQueen said tensely. "But we believe he may have been using another alias, George Palmer, a police officer with Scotland Yard's political investigation department, an antiterrorist organization of the sixties. Palmer disappeared about two years before Jessup showed up with the SIS."

"Are you sure Palmer and Jessup are both Burov?" Gary Manning inquired.

"We're not certain," McQueen replied. "You see, Jessup had undergone cosmetic surgery, supposedly after a nasty fire in which his car was wrecked. We believe the real Wilford Jessup was disposed of by the KGB and replaced by Burov. Jessup had been a member of the Special Military

Intelligence department before the accident. Burov's physical appearance was close enough to pass as either man with some clever facial alterations.''

"What about fingerprints?'' Rafael Encizo inquired.

"Jessup's prints were supposedly destroyed by the fire,'' McQueen answered. "His fingers were allegedly burned too badly. The British should have realized something was odd about that story, but you know how the limeys are.''

"Bloody dreadful, aren't they?'' David McCarter commented dryly. "Well, how did we dumb Brits figure out Jessup was really Burov?''

"A Russian defector betrayed Burov,'' McQueen answered. "Otherwise, London may have never realized the guy was a mole. Fortunately for the British, Burov hadn't been in a position to know much and, at the time, they did not know that the real Jessup had been murdered. So they simply kicked his ass back to Mother Russia. That's when our sources in the Soviet Union learned Burov's true identity. Son of a bitch was awarded the Order of the Red Flag and promoted to light colonel.''

"Let's see what you've got on this dude,'' Calvin James said.

McQueen handed him the file. The black man gazed down at the pleasant smile on Vladimir Burov's face. The man in the photograph appeared to be a middle-aged white who could have been almost any nationality. One might guess he was a businessman or the vice-president of a bank. James passed the photo and file on to Manning.

"Burov must be a very good operative to have successfully passed as a British citizen for so long,'' Katz mused. "He must speak flawless English and know customs and behavior very well. We'd better assume he's well versed in American customs, also. Burov might very well be in charge of the KGB squad we're seeking.''

"You mean seeking us,'' McCarter commented. "Personally, I prefer being the hunter to the hunted.''

"Do you fellows mind telling us who you are and what department you're with?'' Nazarov asked. "This has all been so rushed and so hush-hush I'm not sure who I'm working with except Queenie here.''

He tilted a thumb at McQueen. The NSA man was a big, well-muscled athlete who appeared to pump iron when he was not spying on Soviet embassies. He obviously did not like being called ''Queenie,'' especially by a CIA operative.

''I'm afraid we can't give you any more details than your agencies already gave you,'' Katz replied. ''But you can be sure we're all working on the same side.''

''That'd be a switch,'' McQueen muttered, glaring at Nazarov. ''Anyway, I've got some more material here on lesser-ranking KGB agents who have been shuffling through the UN and Soviet embassies. None of them are as impressive as Burov. Take a look at them if you want.''

''Jesus,'' Nazarov whispered when he glimpsed a photo on another folder. ''Let me see that.''

''Recognize someone?'' Manning asked, handing the folder to the CIA agent.

''Yeah,'' Nazarov confirmed when he examind the file more closely. ''This guy isn't KGB, Queenie. You'd better tell your records people to get their heads out of their assholes. This is Leonid Potapov.''

''GRU?'' Katz guessed, aware that Nazarov had infiltrated the Soviet army while he was a mole behind the iron curtain and had successfully burrowed into military intelligence for more than a year.

''That's right.'' Nazarov nodded. ''I met Potapov. He's a good officer, concerned about his men, plenty of brains and lots of guts. He was popular with most of us because we all knew he gave lip service to the glories of the Communist party, but he really hates those Red slobs in the Kremlin.''

''That made him popular with the GRU?'' Calvin James asked with surprise.

''GRU isn't KGB,'' Nazarov explained. ''Military intelligence is chosen from the ranks of the Soviet army. A lot of GRU officers aren't Communists. Most KGB agents are Reds, but they're still outside the great powers of the party. The politburo, the KGB and the army run the Soviet Union, but they don't have much love for one another. The army is low man on the totem pole and they know it. Maybe the politburo and the KGB are full of real sons of bitches, but the average Russian soldier is just serving his country in uniform. Most of them don't like what the government does, but they can't do much about that.''

"None of us can do much about government," Encizo said with a shrug. "And nobody approves of everything his government does.''

"True," Katz said. "But in some governments at least you can vote politicians into or out of office. You can lawfully assemble without fear of police raiding your group, and you can criticize the ruling powers without winding up in a labor camp.''

"I've always wondered why the Russian people don't form a revolution and throw out the Communists as they did the czar," James commented.

"How can you organize a revolution when you can't get two hundred people together without winding up with at least one KGB agent or a KGB informer in the group?" Nazarov replied. "Don't forget, Lenin set up the Communist power structure in the Soviet Union. He knew all about revolutions and he did his best to safeguard against them.''

"Okay," McQueen said. "So we know Burov and Potapov are in the country and may or may not be connected with whatever you guys are concerned with. I don't know how much good that does. I'm afraid the last we learned about those two, they were in New York City. Damned if they didn't manage to sneak out undetected. We don't know where they got to...yet.''

"So much for the all-seeing eye of the NSA," Nazarov snorted with contempt.

"We'll find them," McQueen insisted. "It's just a matter of time. They're probably traveling with forged ID, but we've set up watch posts at all major airports throughout the country.''

"Assuming they decided to travel by regular airlines," McCarter added as he popped open a can of Coca Cola. "They could be anywhere by now and teamed up with other Soviet agents planning their next move.''

The telephone in the conference room rang. It was an in-house line, which meant the call was from the hotel switch-board. Katz answered the phone and identified himself by his cover name, Howard Goldberg.

"Mr. Goldberg," the voice of the desk clerk began. "There's a telephone call for you. The caller says it's urgent."

"Put the call through," the Israeli replied.

"Yes, sir," the clerk answered.

"Goldberg?" Hal Brognola's voice asked.

"Yes," Katz answered.

"Turn on the TV and watch the news," Brognola instructed. "I think you'll be interested in the report on how our stock is doing."

"Indeed," the Phoenix Force commander replied. "I have a couple of potential investors present. Do you think this information is relevant to them?"

"They'll find out about it anyway," the Fed replied. "It's not a state secret. It's on national TV, for chrissake. They might not put one and one together as quickly as you will, but we'll want those new investors' help anyway."

"I understand," Katz assured him.

"Good luck," Brognola said and hung up.

"Turn on the televison set and find a news broadcast," Katz said, putting the phone receiver in the cradle. "CBN if they've got it."

Encizo switched on the small color TV mounted to a wall. They watched a news story about an outbreak of violence in the Middle East, followed by a report about a horrendous massacre in Georgia. Heinz Muller, described as an "eccentric adventurer," and eleven members of his "right-wing paramilitary organization" had been killed in a gun battle with unidentified assailants. The survivalist camp had apparently been attacked by someone armed with automatic weapons and explosives. There were no suspects although someone had painted "Kill Whitey" across the sign in front of the camp. Police were looking into the possibility that a militant black group might be involved.

"There is not ample evidence at this time to say anything for certain," a reporter announced grimly. "But this could be the beginning of racial tensions worse than anything that happened in the sixties...."

"He sounds as if he'd like to see a race war," McCarter muttered with disgust. "Those media vultures make me sick."

"Race wars make great news stories," James said with a grin. "That dude's just trying to drum up a little business, man."

"Is this business in Georgia supposed to be connected with the KGB?" McQueen frowned. "If so, I don't see—"

"Heinz Muller was a professional mercenary who worked for both the CIA and the British secret service in the past," Katz explained. "He was roughly my age and build and he only had one hand."

The Israeli held up the trident-hook device at the end of his prosthetic arm.

"You think the KGB was looking for you and they killed Muller by mistake?" McQueen rolled his eyes toward the ceiling. "Come on, Goldberg, or whatever your name really is. We're talking about the KGB, damn it. They aren't that careless."

"I wouldn't accuse them of being careless," Katz replied. "But they don't care if they kill a few innocent bystanders to accomplish a mission. Muller may have been the man they wanted and they certainly regarded him as an enemy. So they killed him."

"But to carry out a full-scale slaughter just isn't their style," McQueen insisted.

"It isn't their style in *this country*," Katz corrected. "The KGB has been involved in atrocities committed within the Soviet Union, especially when it was still the NKVD under Stalin. They've been responsible for massacres in Africa, Central America and Afghanistan. The only reason they haven't participated in outright slaughter in the United States is because they've had to keep a low profile and they've lacked sufficient manpower."

"And they're not concerned about a low profile now?" Nazarov inquired.

"They're more arrogant because they have the manpower now," the Phoenix Force commander explained. "The KGB has command of a unit of commandos. Perhaps a *large* unit of commandos. Besides, how great is the risk? Who would associate the raid and slaughter of a washed up mercenary and his survivalist students with the KGB?"

"Some people will think the place was attacked by militant blacks," James added. "Others will figure correctly that the 'Kill Whitey' message was meant to throw investigators off the track. Hell, Charles Manson did the same thing with the Tate-LaBianca killings. But even the folks who see through the smoke screen will probably be looking for a paramilitary outfit similar to what Muller was running. They'll assume the competition had him offed."

"When they look into the guy's background and find out he'd once been hired by the CIA, the circus will really begin," Gary Manning commented. "You'll probably hear conspiracy theories about why the CIA or FBI would want to kill Muller. Maybe they'll even come up with a theory that Muller may have been planning to invade Cuba and Castro had him killed. But nobody will point a finger at Moscow. You can be sure of that."

"Except you guys," McQueen said. "I'm not convinced you're right."

"Then let's try to get some proof," Katz suggested. "You said the NSA has watch posts set up at all major airports, right? Contact them and tell them to watch for individuals who are leaving Georgia. If they have access to airport security cameras, then try to get film or videotape of any passengers who left since the Muller incident. The KGB won't remain in the state after this happened."

"But where will they go next?" McQueen began. "You're so smart, why don't you answer that question?"

"They'll flee Georgia and either head for another state or flee the country," the Israeli answered. "If they do the latter, the Russians will head for Florida or the Mexican border and try to get to Cuba. Then they'll be heading back to the USSR, and that's the end of our problems for now."

"If they go to another state?" Nazarov asked.

"Then they'll plot out their next plan of action and try again," Katz replied simply. "And I suspect that's the path they'll take. Moscow is obviously risking too much with this mission not to make it very clear to whoever is in charge that failure will mean death. The KGB isn't going to give up so easily."

"My guess is they'll head to an area two or three states away from Georgia," Manning added. "Probably wind up in Kentucky or Mississippi. Maybe even Texas."

"Why not run to California or Alaska?" McQueen asked with a shrug. "Wouldn't they want to get as far away as possible?"

"Sure they would," Encizo supplied the answer. "But the KGB has a bunch of Russian soldiers with them. Most of those guys probably don't speak English well enough to travel openly without attracting attention. Some of the elite KGB might fly out of state, but the rest will have to travel by truck or perhaps even by bus. The point is, they won't be able to run too far too fast and they'll need to regroup and plan what to do next."

"That's an awful lot of assumptions," McQueen said, shaking his head. "I don't know how you can hope to second-guess these jokers."

"And you might be barking up the wrong tree anyway," Nazarov added. "Maybe Muller wasn't hit by the KGB."

"Perhaps not," Katz admitted, "But unless someone else has another lead for us to check out, this is all we have to go on."

"I'll tell you what," McQueen began. "If I hadn't received orders directly from the office of the director to co-operate with you guys in every matter possible..."

"Skip it, bloke," McCarter cut him off. "What's important is that you *are* under orders to do what we say, so just shut up and do it."

11

"Can I pluck the feathers off first?" Dashiell McQueen asked when he met with Phoenix Force the following day.

"Pluck the feathers from what?" Rafael Encizo replied, confused by the NSA man's remark.

"Before I have to eat crow," McQueen explained as he opened his briefcase. "Looks like you fellas were right and I was wrong."

"We're all on the same side, Mr. McQueen," Yakov Katzenelenbogen assured him. "So don't worry about that."

"At least that CIA asshole Nazarov was wrong, too," McQueen said with a shrug. "Anyway, we checked out airport security tapes for about two hundred different locations and damned if we didn't come up with a Russian in the woodpile."

"Cute expression," Calvin James said dryly. "Who did you guys find and where is he?"

"A fella calling himself Harold Graves bought a ticket in cash for a first-class seat aboard South Central airlines Flight 223 from Atlanta to Houston, Texas," the NSA agent explained. "He's been identified as Colonel Vladimir Burov. A couple of points of interest: Burov spoke English with a British accent and he was accompanied by another man using the name Thomas Simon. We don't have anything on file about the guy, but I think it's safe to assume he's probably KGB, too."

"First class, eh?" Gary Manning mused. "Burov must like traveling in style. Was there anyone else interesting on board Flight 223?"

"You guessed it," McQueen replied. "We identified two lesser KGB agents among the coach ticket holders. Pretty good chance there were more Russkies among the passengers we failed to identify."

"So the KGB has decided to set up camp in Houston," Encizo mused, gazing at a wall map of the United States. "Why did they pick Houston?"

"Perhaps they just needed a place to meet and plan their next move," Manning suggested.

"Or they might be trying to get across the border into Mexico," the Cuban stated. "Mexico has been a favorite port of entry for Soviet spies since the days of the NKVD. It's no secret that *federales* and *politicos* can be bribed fairly easily in Mexico."

"Isn't that a rather biased remark?" McQueen asked. "I've seen how the KGB has been shuffling through the United Nations and Soviet embassies for years. Christ, some of them have purchased summer homes in California and winter homes in Florida. It's no wonder the KGB can get more information about us than we can about them."

"That's true." Encizo nodded. "But it's also true that Mexico has long been a bus station for the KGB. If they don't like that reputation, then they'd better do something about it instead of pretending the KGB doesn't exist."

"Trouble is, most of the free world has been pretty good at ignoring the Soviets' covert activities," David McCarter stated as he began pacing the floor. "Tell you what, mate, I've been involved in antiterrorist activity for about fifteen years, and you can trace most of the trouble back to Moscow. Nobody wants to admit that, of course. Everybody wants peace and folks figure détente and Salt and Start treaties sound lovely, but the bloody KGB doesn't play by our rules."

"I'm no Commie lover," McQueen responded, "but they aren't the only bastards involved in international terrorism.

Look at Iran and Libya. Even the CIA sent a terrorist manual to so-called freedom fighters in Nicaragua."

"You're referring to Field Manual 95-1A," Katzenelenbogen declared. "Which is a guerrilla war manual, also referred to as a 'psychological operations for guerrilla warfare manual.' Have you read it, Mr. McQueen?"

"Well, no," the NSA man admitted.

"I have," Katz told him. "It's an instruction manual concerning basic guerrilla warfare tactics. The media made a big stink about it but, few of its critics have actually read it. They ought to. It does not give great detail about murder or sabotage. Most important, it emphasizes protecting innocent lives and choosing targets with utmost care. That's the difference between guerrilla warfare and terrorism. A terrorist wants a large body count. He is in the business of creating terror and murdering innocent bystanders. A genuine guerrilla fighter may use violence, but his targets are selected with care. The Field Manual 95-1A is certainly no more a terrorist handbook than Mao Tse-tung's *Little Red Book*."

"If you want to read a terrorist handbook," Encizo suggested, "get your hands on a copy of Carlos Marighella's *Mini-Manual for Urban Guerrillas*. It tells you all about how to kill innocent people for theatrical effect and it quotes Lenin when it states 'the purpose of terror is to terrorize.'"

"This is a great discussion," Calvin James remarked. "But I think we'd better continue it later. Right now, let's haul ass to Houston and try to find out what the KGB is up to."

"That's the kind of logic that is difficult to argue with," Manning said with a nod.

THANKS TO STONY MAN'S PRESIDENTIAL AUTHORITY, Phoenix Force had no trouble getting a flight from North Dakota to Texas. Phoenix Force and Dashiell McQueen boarded an Air Force C-130 at the Minot Air Base. Their top-secret clearance allowed the special commando unit to avoid any searches and thus carry all the weapons and equipment they desired. The plane arrived at Randolph Air Base near San Antonio where the same airtight security allowed them to leave the base with no questions asked.

Phoenix Force and McQueen joined Sidney Nazarov in San Antonio. The CIA case officer had flown to Texas on an earlier flight to coordinate a combined unit of Central Intelligence Agency and National Security Agency personnel. Not surprisingly, the CIA and NSA agents were less than happy to be working together.

The safehouse for the operation was in the back room of a furniture store in downtown San Antonio. When Phoenix Force entered the room, they found the four CIA agents and three NSA operatives seated on opposite sides of the room, resembling a pair of street gangs prepared for a Saturday-night rumble. The NSA seemed relieved that McQueen had arrived. This evened the odds with the CIA.

"Thank God we didn't get assistance from the FBI, too," Manning whispered to Katz. "Then we'd have a three-way battle to deal with."

"I don't think we could handle much more help from the federal government," the Israeli agreed.

"My name is Kovaks," a short, dark-haired man with a mandarin mustache announced. "NSA. I understand you men are in charge."

"That's right," Katz confirmed. "What have you got for us, Mr. Kovaks?"

"There's a man calling himself Fredrick Clarke who arrived on Flight 223 from Atlanta yesterday morning," Kovaks began. "This CIA joker claims Clarke is supposed to be a Russian agent..."

"Wait a minute," Nazarov declared. "That was a conclusion the NSA came up with based on their surveillance of the Soviet embassy personnel. Ask McQueen if you don't believe me."

"All right," Katz said sharply, weary of the bickering between the NSA and CIA. "Mr. McQueen, is this Fredrick Clarke a KGB agent?"

"According to our records," McQueen began, "Clarke is really Antoli Metkov, a member of the KGB foreign service."

"Thank you," the Israeli said. "Now, Mr. Kovaks, let's hear what you've found out about this man."

"Well, Clarke, or whatever his name is, checked into a Holiday Inn and then headed east of Houston to a string of warehouses," Kovaks explained. "The guy rented one of the buildings. Pretty good sized warehouse."

"Big enough to park a large truck inside?" Encizo inquired.

"It'd handle an eighteen wheeler with no problem," Kovaks confirmed with a nod. "You figure the Russians are having something delivered by truck?"

"That's what we figure," James answered.

"What are the Russians bringing into the state?" Kovaks asked.

"More Russians," James told him. "Speaking of other Russians, did you guys manage to keep track of any of the other KGB dudes who got off Flight 223?"

"We're especially interested in Colonel Burov," Manning added. "The one claiming to be Harold Graves."

"He checked in the Hilton Hotel along with that Simon guy," Kovaks explained. "I guess he's supposed to be a KGB agent, too?"

"God, you learn fast," Nazarov snorted with disgust.

"I trust you've got surveillance teams watching the warehouse and the hotels?" Katz asked quickly, trying to cut off another argument.

"Naturally," Kovaks assured him. "You think we're stupid or something?"

"Something," one of the CIA agents muttered.

"Gentlemen," Katz began wearily. "Let's just concentrate on the Soviets for now. The CIA and NSA can go back to quarreling after this mission is over."

"Right now," Manning began, "I think we'd better get to Houston and take a look at this situation for ourselves. Since the Soviets have split up, I think it's probable that

Burov and his companion suspect that they might be under surveillance. That means they'll probably stay put for a while.''

"We've got their phone tapped," Kovaks declared. "And there's an electronic listening device installed in one of the walls.''

"How'd you manage that?" Nazarov asked with surprise. "You didn't know which room they'd take or even which hotel.''

"The tap was easy," Kovaks explained. "We just tapped the direct line into the hotel itself. When the terminal registers a room number, we just switch over to the Ivan's room if he calls out. The eavesdropping device was a little trickier. A couple of our agents picked the lock to the room next to Graves's. Then they found a wall that connected to the Russians' suite, removed a picture and drilled a hole large enough to insert a limpet mike. It's wireless, of course, activated by the sound of voices from the subject's room. It transmits a special low-frequency radio signal to a receiver in the possession of the hotel surveillance team.''

"Very clever," Nazarov said with an approving nod.

"Thanks." Kovaks smiled. "We NSA guys try to do our best.''

"You've done a good job," Katz agreed. "But I wouldn't count on wiretaps or hidden microphones when you're dealing with the KGB. If Burov and his partner suspect they're being watched, they'll be very careful about what they say while they're in that hotel room. Don't forget, these fellows are from the Soviet Union and part of the largest intelligence outfit in the world. They're accustomed to spying on their own people and assuming someone else is spying on them.''

"Those fuckers must be as paranoid as hell," McQueen commented.

"Aren't we all?" McCarter chuckled. "And don't we all have good reason to be?''

"This job's getting weird, man," Calvin James muttered.

"You noticed that, huh?" Encizo replied dryly.

12

Anyone who thinks Texas is all ranch country and cowboys has never seen the Houston skyline, visible from the freeway as one enters the city. It is a breathtaking view dominated by the superpowers of the oil business. The great monolith of One Shell Plaza, with its enormous antenna extending from the roof, and the majestic twin towers of Pennzoil Place are giants of steel, concrete and glass.

But the men of Phoenix Force had not come to Houston to see the sights. They could enjoy little more than an intriguing glimpse of this marvelous city as they rode in the back of a Volkswagen Mini-Bus driven by a CIA agent named Connors. The traffic was heavy and fast, reminiscent of the autobahn in West Germany.

The Mini-Bus pulled onto Prairie Street and headed southeast. Phoenix Force had decided to concentrate on the warehouse rented by the KGB since the eavesdropping devices in Burov's hotel room had not produced any results. Agent Connors pulled onto a narrow road bisecting rows of warehouses, resembling a cluster of old airplane hangars.

One warehouse opened its sliding doors when the bus arrived, and Connors steered the VW inside the building. Two men inside the warehouse quickly pushed the doors shut. As Phoenix Force emerged from the vehicle, a short, immensely fat man waddled forward. A wide grin stretched from one side of his broad round face to the other as he mopped his brow with a sweat-stained handkerchief.

"How do, gents," the fat man greeted with an East Texas drawl. "They call me the Warlock. I understand you're here to do somethin' about those godless Commies we got stayin' on this block.''

"I'm afraid you're ahead of us," Katz replied. "We knew that a KGB agent rented one of these warehouses, but no one told us there was anyone in the building.''

"Well, there wasn't," the Warlock chuckled. "Until a big old truck 'bout the size of an army deuce and a half pulled into here twenty minutes ago. Know what they brung in that truck?''

"We just got here, remember?" Calvin James replied dryly.

"Tell you what they brung, boy," the Warlock's eyes hardened when he turned toward the black man. "They brung 'bout two-and-a-half tons of Russians in that rig. And I don't mean no black Russians. You know, like the drink?''

"I surely do, Mistah Warlock, suh," James said with his best "step and fetch it" imitation. "Now, how do you know what's inside that warehouse, fella? Did you creep over there and wiggle through the keyhole?''

"I was told you boys was professionals," the Warlock remarked. "Hope none of you got your job by affirmative action, if you know what I mean.''

"Oh, we know what you mean," David McCarter said angrily. "And how'd you like my boot up your fat arse?''

"Relax, Masters," James told McCarter, using the Briton's cover name. "The Warlock is just joshin' us, man. He doesn't really mind the shade of my skin any more than I mind his red neck.''

"That's right." The Warlock smiled. "I'm just funnin'.''

"We don't have time for jokes or petty bigotries, Warlock," Katz said gruffly. "Now, what proof do you have that there are Russians in that warehouse?''

"I'm what they call an electronics surveillance expert, fella," the Warlock stated. "When I tell you somethin', you can bet your sweet ass I know what I'm talkin' about.''

"You sure as hell haven't proved it to us so far," Rafael Encizo remarked.

"Is that right, amigo?" The Warlock glared at Encizo. "Well, you fellas come along with the Warlock and I'll show you somethin' to make believers out of you. *Comprende*?"

The Warlock led Phoenix Force to a small office connected to the main bay area. In the center of the room stood a strange contraption mounted on a tripod similar to that used by professional photographers. Instead of a camera, a series of aluminum tubes were mounted to the tripod on metal brackets. A cone-shaped device was fitted at the end of the outfit with a wire extending to a special amplifier on a table. Seated at the table was another NSA surveillance man wearing a set of headphones hooked up to the amplifier. A cassette tape recorder was also connected to the device.

"Any of you multiracial professionals happen to know what this is?" the Warlock inquired smugly.

"Sure," Gary Manning said with a shrug. "It's a rifle microphone. The aluminum tubes act as wave guides to increase the reception capabilities of an ultrasensitive microphone in the base of the rig. Big deal. Hate to tell you this, Warlock, but this thing is a goddamn dinosaur compared to modern state-of-the-art equipment."

"Oh?" Warlock smiled. "You mean shit like laser projection devices and super-duper transistorized microphones disguised as olives in martini glasses or plastic flies stuck to the wall that can send a signal to an infinity transmitter? Look, sonny, I've used that fancy stuff and a lot of high-tech crap you never heard of. Let me tell you somethin', most of it is just that. Crap. Those lasers and teeny-weeny transistors are unreliable. Half the time they don't function right and even when they do, they're not any better than this baby."

He pointed a stubby finger at the rifle microphone. Katz examined the device and noticed it was pointed at a window that had its shade drawn. The Phoenix Force commander was not an authority on surveillance equipment, but he knew that the rifle microphone was only practical for listening in on conversations approximately twenty to fifty yards away. That meant the KGB warehouse was close. Very close.

"All right, Warlock," Katz declared. "We're about as impressed as you're going to get us. Now let's hear some proof."

"Sure enough," the Warlock agreed as he pressed the Rewind button on the tape recorder. "Listen to this."

He punched the Play button and the recorder uttered a scratchy hum. The reception was not crystal clear, but voices were unmistakable among the static.

"Shto yah dolzhun d'eluht?" a recorded voice asked.

"Po-ee-domt'eh som-noy," another voice commanded.

"There," Warlock said, switching off his machine. "Now, I don't speak no Russian, but I reckon that's what language they was speakin'."

"I rather hate to say this, Warlock," Katz remarked, "but you're right."

"What were the Russians talking about, Mr. Goldberg?" Manning asked, referring to Katz by his cover name.

"Nothing very exciting," the Israeli replied. "One fellow asked what he was supposed to do and the other said to come with him. We can only guess what they're talking about and we'd probably guess wrong."

"Guessin' about things ain't my job, Mr. Gold-Jew," the Warlock said with a sneer. "You boys is a regular United Nations, ain't you?"

"How did a fat, smart-mouth bastard like you manage to live so long?" McCarter snarled, hands balled into fists that he was obviously eager to use.

"Calm down, Masters," Katz urged. "If you've finished your job, Warlock, I think you'd better get out of here before somebody loses his temper."

"Sure enough." The Warlock grinned. "You boys have fun with the Russians. By the way, I free-lance. Maybe next time, I'll be listenin' in on you."

"Sure hope the NSA pays you enough to get a personality transplant, fella," James told the Warlock.

The surveillance expert waddled into the bay area as agent Connors entered the room. He raised his shoulders in an apologetic shrug.

"Sorry about that bastard," he told the men of Phoenix Force. "The Warlock is a real son of a bitch, but he's also one of the best electronic surveillance men in the business."

"No need to apologize for him," Katz assured the CIA agent.

"What makes it worse is that Warlock is a Texan," Connors added. "Same as I am...."

"I don't think the two of you have anything in common," Encizo remarked.

"Well," Connors said lamely, "I just didn't want you to think all Texans are like him."

"Don't worry about it," James said. "Making generalizations about people based on geography is another brand of bigotry. That's the Warlock's bag, not our's."

"Speaking of our bag," Katz added, "we'd better get back to the business at hand. How do we handle the Soviet agents in that warehouse?"

"It must be the building next to this one, right?" Manning asked the NSA surveillance man still seated at the table.

"That's right, sir," the agent replied. "They're about a hundred and twenty feet from this room."

"Any idea how many guys are in there?" the Canadian inquired.

"I'm not sure," the NSA man admitted. "It's hard to tell their voices apart with this rifle phone, and not understanding Russian doesn't help. But I've heard a number of footfalls coming from that building. I figure there're at least twenty guys in there."

"Jesus," Connors rasped. "We'd better call in some reinforcements."

"No way," Encizo told him. "If we bring in a bunch of CIA and NSA guys those Russians are going to come out shooting. We'll have a full-scale gun battle all over this area. Too many things could go wrong. Some of the Russians might escape, bystanders could get killed and the Soviets might force us to shoot them all down.''

"We need at least one or two of them alive," Manning added. "You can't interrogate a corpse."

"Then what can we do?" Connors asked.

"Contact Nazarov and McQueen," Katz instructed, taking a Seiko chronometer from his pocket. "It is now 1745 hours. By 1830 hours we want this area blacked out."

"Blacked out?" The CIA man frowned.

"An electrical blackout," Katz explained. "I want all electricity within a least four blocks to be cut off. I don't care if they have to shut off power for the whole city, but I want a blackout for this area at 1830 exactly. Understand?"

"Then what?" Connors asked, confused and more than a little frightened by these five hard-ass mystery men.

"Then you blokes just stay out of the way," McCarter said with a wolfish grin. "And let us do what we do best, mate."

13

Phoenix Force had less than an hour to prepare for the raid on the enemy warehouse. Yakov Katzenelenbogen listened to the tapes that had been recorded with the rifle microphone. The KGB conversations inside the warehouse consisted of little more than instructions for setting up equipment.

However, Katz did learn a few valuable details. The Russians referred to a radio. Unless they were exceptionally fond of country and western music, this suggested they had a transceiver that would allow them to get in touch with other Soviet operatives. One of the Russians also mentioned a generator, which could mean the KGB had brought along an emergency power source. This was less than welcome news.

The five-men army made certain all their weapons were ready for combat. Katz and McCarter would use their favorite firearms, an Uzi subgun and SIG-Sauer pistol for the Israeli and an M-10 Ingram and Browning Hi-Power autoloader for the Briton. McCarter regarded combat as the most honest of human activities. Politics and lies are not part of actual combat. The battlefield has a primitive purity. It is survival, plain and simple.

Gary Manning selected a Remington shotgun with a SWAT-style folding stock for the raid. The Canadian rifle champ liked a shotgun for close-quarters fighting, where buckshot was just as deadly as full-auto bullets. Manning had Dutch loaded the magazine with double O buck and 12GA/500 Sabot bullets, the latter having the range and penetrating force of a high-powered rifle slug.

Calvin James favored an M-16 assault rifle for most operations, but tonight's mission would be at close quarters so he chose a Smith & Wesson M-76 submachine gun. The 9mm chatterbox was a favorite of the SEALSs. The black warrior also carried a Colt Commander in a Jackass Leather shoulder rig. The big .45-caliber pistol was in a holster under his left arm and a G-96 Jet-Aer fighting dagger was clipped to the harness under his right.

Rafael Encizo, like McCarter, was a close-quarters fighter. His Heckler & Koch MP-5 was designed for ultimate devastation at close range. The Cuban also carried a S&W Model 59 double-action automatic in a hip holster and an old friend, the Walther PPK, in a shoulder rig for backup. In addition to the firepower, Encizo wore a Cold Steel Tanto fighting knife in a belt sheath and a Gerber Mark I combat dagger in an ankle scabbard. A leather pouch on his belt contained three *shaken* throwing stars. Encizo was an expert in the art of *shuriken-jitsu*, a skill he first learned from the late Keio Ohara and that he continued to develop.

The five men were also equipped with M-17 gas masks, an assortment of tear gas canisters, SAS "flash-bang" stun grenades, and Nitefinder infrared headsets. McCarter, Manning and James each had a Bio-Inoculator, a large air pistol that fires a tranquilizer dart. James, the unit medic and chemist, had loaded each dart with two hundred fifty milligrams of Thorazine, more than enough to put a man in dreamland, but not enough to put him six feet under. All five men of Phoenix Force and their CIA and NSA allies sat in the dark, having switched off the lights at dusk to avoid betraying their presence to the KGB in the nearby warehouse.

Agent Conners turned to Katzenelenbogen. The Israeli's face was barely visible, but the glow of a burning Camel cigarette in his mouth made him easier to recognize than most of the others. McCarter was puffing on a Players. Encizo waved wisps of cigarette smoke away from his face and muttered something about lung cancer.

"You shouldn't go in there alone," Connors insisted. "The odds are too great...."

"We've faced greater odds in the past," Katz assured him. "Besides, there's no other way. We've already explained that."

"I've got 1830 hours, damn it," McCarter announced, looking at the luminous face of his Le Grand wristwatch. "We should have our blackout any second...unless McQueen and Nazarov are too busy fighting with each other to do their bloody job."

"Take it easy," Manning urged as he peered out a window. As he watched, lamps outside blinked out and the surrounding area was pitch-black. "That's it! Lights out!"

"About bloody time," McCarter muttered, unable to resist a final complaint.

The five men of Phoenix Force donned their Nitefinder headsets, gathered their weapons and hurried from the building. They had discussed the plan of action and each man knew where he was supposed to go and what he was supposed to do.

The raid on the enemy base had begun.

Katz, Encizo and Manning headed for the rear of the KGB warehouse while James and McCarter moved to the front entrance. They heard voices barking orders in Russian, muffled by the walls of the building. Boot leather slapped the concrete floors inside the warehouse; obviously the Soviets did not intend to just sit down in the dark, light some candles and wait for the power to come on. Phoenix Force quickly moved into position, aware that their opponents would not be off-balance for long.

Drab yellow light appeared at the windows as an electrical hum vibrated throughout the building. The Russians had switched on emergency generators. Phoenix Force quickly removed their Nitefinder goggles, aware that bright light could blind them if they kept the infrared headsets on.

The front door opened and two Russians dressed in dark trousers and jackets stepped outside. Both men carried Stechin machine pistols.

The Russians moved ___ cautiously, trying to determine how much of the city ha___ ___en affected by the blackout, and ready for trouble. McC___ E___ and James, positioned on each side of the building, st___ ___ out of sight behind the corners of the warehouse.

Calvin James took ___ ___ll pebble from his pocket and flicked it with a thum___ ___ ___ss the tiny projectile onto the road. The faint sound ___ ___ pebble striking pavement drew the attention of the tw___ ___et gunmen.

One of the Russians ___ ___ered something and both men slowly moved toward ___ ___nd, approaching James's position. McCarter liste___ ___ their footfalls and carefully peered around the co___ ___ aimed the BI pistol carefully, using the luminous fr___ ___ ___ear sights to train the weapon in the dim light. The ___ ___pistol champ squeezed the trigger. The Bio-Inocula___ ___sed like a serpent as it fired a feathered projectile.

The hypodart stru___ ___ ___e of the Soviet agents in the nape of the neck, and Th___ ___ine was immediately injected into the man's bloodstre___ ___ The Russian groaned and slapped a hand to the back ___ ___ ___is neck, plucking the dart from his flesh.

He rasped a word ___ ___owing the dart to his comrade, then the drugged Russian ___ ___nees buckled and he fell to all fours. The other Soviet op___ ___tive turned toward McCarter's position, switching the s___ ___ctor switch of his Stechin to full-auto.

Calvin James stru___ ___ without warning. He lashed the steel barrel of his M-76 ___submachine gun across the Russian's wrist, knocking the ___techin from stunned fingers. The black warrior then whip___ed the S&W subgun into the startled Russian's face. Th___ blow staggered the Soviet against the wall, and James i___mediately hammered the butt of the folding stock into the man's abdomen. The Russian doubled up with a groan and James expertly rabbit punched his opponent with a well-placed karate chop to the mastoid bone. The Soviet flunky collapsed to the ground with a sigh as consciousness slipped from his body.

The drugged Russian gazed up at James and awkwardly tried to raise his machine pistol. The Thorazine made his muscles heavy and his movement was sluggish and clumsy. James easily kicked the Stechin from the man's hands and rapped him lightly on the temple with a back-fist stroke. The Soviet fell on his side and slipped into dreamland at last.

A third Russian charged through the doorway, jacking the slide of a Makarov to chamber a 9mm round. His attention was locked on Calvin James. The Soviet did not even know McCarter was present until it was too late. The Briton dashed around the corner and lashed out a boot, kicking the Russian hard in the gut. The man folded with a grunt as McCarter swung the M-10 Ingram with a backhand sweep, striking the Makarov from his opponent's hand.

McCarter moved in a circular pattern favored by Chinese martial artists and whipped his left fist across the Russian's jaw. The Soviet dropped in a stunned lump as two more Russians dashed toward the doorway, weapons held ready. McCarter fired his Ingram machine pistol, holding the M-10 in his right fist. A volley of parabellum rounds chopped into the chest of an advancing Russian and hurled the guy backward into his comrade.

The Briton jumped away from the door and Calvin James opened up with his M-76, firing another salvo of 9mm hellstones across the warehouse threshold. At least one Russian was struck as a voice shrieked in reply. McCarter quickly took an SAS "flash-bang" grenade from his belt and pulled the pin. The British ace held the blaster for two seconds and tossed it through the doorway.

The Phoenix pair stood clear of the door and covered their ears as the concussion grenade exploded. The blast seemed to send a tremble through the building as a flash of brilliant white light burst through the doorway. James gathered up one of the fallen Stechin machine pistols and tossed it to McCarter. Then he picked up the other Soviet blast machine for himself.

"What the hell, man," James chuckled. "They're free."

AT THE REAR of the warehouse Gary Manning had inserted a small CV-38 charge near the lock to the back door. The low-boom RDX plastic explosive efficiently blew the door open, barely scratching the frame. Yakov Katzenelenbogen immediately fired a quick burst from his Uzi, pumping a stream of 9mm rounds into a horrified Russian who ran straight into the 3-round spray of death. Encizo tossed in a second concussion grenade, and the Phoenix Force trio stood away from the door and allowed the SAS stun bomb to do its job.

The second blast rocked the building, and windows exploded, sending glass fragments and splintered framework hurtling outside. Katz, Manning and Encizo charged inside the warehouse, staying low because they knew James and McCarter would enter with guns blazing.

McCarter and James did not disappoint them. The Briton burst through the front door with his Ingram in one hand and the borrowed Stechin in the other. His black partner entered with his M-76 subgun braced against his right hip and the other Russian machine pistol in his left fist. All four weapons blasted full-auto destruction into the dazed and horrified Soviet agents within the warehouse.

Of course, firing full-auto weapons in this manner reduced accuracy to virtually zero, but the number of 9mm rounds that rocketed through the interior of the warehouse was incredible. Within less than three seconds, James and McCarter fired more than fifty parabellum projectiles. Most of the bullets struck the body and cab of a tractor-trailer rig in the middle of the bay area. Others slammed into the walls of the building, and at least three Russians were hit by the furious rain of copper-jacketed death.

The Briton moved to the right while James jumped to the left. McCarter literally ran into a pair of Russians who were dazed but conscious after the double-concussion blasts inside the building. One Soviet quickly grabbed McCarter's right forearm and wrenched violently, forcing the Ingram from the Briton's fist. The second Soviet was too slow. He tried to seize McCarter's other arm, but the British war machine triggered the Stechin and drilled three 9mm rounds through the Russian's chest.

Still grappling with McCarter, the first Soviet slashed the side of his hand across the Briton's wrist to strike the Stechin from McCarter's grasp. The Phoenix pro reacted like a cornered tiger. He instantly whipped a knee to his opponent's groin and thrust his skull forward in a vicious head butt. The frontal bone of McCarter's hard cranium nutted the Russian at the bridge of the nose.

The Soviet was staggered by the blow, and blood oozed from his left nostril. McCarter did not give his opponent time to recover. He swung a hard right cross to the Russian's jaw and followed with two fast left jabs, hitting the Kremlin enforcer on the point of the chin and upper lip. The Russian started to sag, and McCarter hit him once more with a kung fu "dragon head" punch. A bent knuckle rammed into the Soviet's solar plexus and the Russian uttered a sickly gasp and crumpled to the floor.

Another Soviet hitman saw McCarter and swung a Skorpion machine pistol at the Briton. McCarter immediately threw himself to the floor, falling to the left as he yanked the Browning Hi-Power from shoulder leather. A stream of 7.65mm bullets spat from the Czech chatterbox, the slugs sizzling through air above McCarter's prone body as he triggered the Browning autoloader. The Briton's pistol snarled twice, pumping two parabellum rounds directly into the Russian's chest, left of center. The Soviet gunman's heart exploded and he was dead before he could feel the hard concrete smack his body.

Calvin James also found the Russians still had plenty of fight left. He shuffled right into a dazed Soviet agent who was on all fours, his eardrums wrecked by the blasts. James tripped and fell on top of the Russian as another Kremlin killer closed in with an AK-74 assault rifle in his fists.

The black hardcase braced his M-76 on the body of the Russian he had landed on and opened fire. Four 9mm slugs tore into the large and small intestines of the enemy rifleman, and the Soviet gunsel screamed as he folded up in agony. James fired another burst from his Smith & Wesson chopper, blasting the life from the Russian.

James felt the man beneath him stir. He had exhausted the ammo from his M-76, so he dropped the subgun and smashed an elbow to the base of the Russian's skull. The man's body went limp as James shuffled the Stechin from his left hand to his right. The black warrior started to rise when a swarm of high-velocity slugs richocheted off the concrete floor less than a yard from his face.

The Phoenix fighter rolled away from the violent sparks and flying chips of concrete and swung the Stechin in the direction of the enemy fire. Positioned on a catwalk, twelve feet above the floor, a Russian with a PPS submachine gun turned his weapon toward the black man.

James fired the Stechin, and a volley of 9mm rounds pelted the catwalk. One stray slug splintered wood from the handrail, but the other punched into human flesh. The Russian gunman cried out as he dropped his subgun and fell heavily against the rail. His body tumbled over the edge and he plunged screaming to the hard floor below.

Yakov Katzenelenbogen and Gary Manning moved toward the rear of the tractor-trailer rig. The big doors of the long box-shaped trailer stood open, and a Russian with an AK-74 suddenly appeared at the edge of the vehicle. Katz snap-aimed his Uzi and blasted the gunman with parabellum slugs. The impact of the multiple high-velocity bullets slammed the guy back behind the trailer to fall lifeless onto the concrete.

Suddenly a KGB agent armed with a Makarov pistol and a Soviet commando packing an American-made M-16 rifle appeared at the open mouth of the trailer. Manning's Remington roared. The double O buck shotgun blast smashed the Russian paratrooper's chest into gory pulp and hurled his corpse back inside the trailer. A few stray pellets tore into the KGB agent's forearm, forcing him to drop his Makarov.

No one could accuse the Committee for State Security agent of cowardice. Unarmed, he dived from the rear of the trailer, launching himself at Katzenelenbogen. The Israeli sidestepped and allowed the Russian to crash-dive to the concrete. The KGB man's body seemed to splat when it hit the floor, yet he slowly tried to rise. Yakov stepped forward and calmly kicked him behind the ear, rendering the Soviet unconscious.

Another pair of Russian gunmen poked weapons from the rear of the trailer and Manning's shotgun bellowed again. Buckshot ripped one Soviet gunsel's torso to bits and hurled him back against the wall of the trailer. The other Russian took a volley of pellets in his upper chest. He staggered and fell, but held on to an M-76 submachine gun. Katz hit the guy with a salvo of Uzi slugs, nearly ripping the Russian's head from his shoulders as 9mm rounds punched through his throat and lower jawbone.

Rafael Encizo found two Soviet agents stationed by a bulky field radio with a tall antenna that extended to the catwalk overhead. One of the KGB boys was wearing a headset and shouting something into a microphone. Encizo did not want to risk damaging the radio, which might help lead Phoenix Force to the location of other Soviet opponents, so he decided against using the H&K machine pistol and drew his S&W M-59 from its holster.

The Russian standing guard by the radio operator spotted Encizo and raised a PPS subgun as the Cuban extended his arms, aiming the M-59 with both hands. Encizo squeezed the trigger and a parabellum round smashed through the Russian's forehead and drilled through his brain to blast a messy exit hole at the back of his skull.

The KGB agent at the radio had been splattered by blood and brain matter and he screamed and jumped away from the machine, snatching up a Makarov pistol from the table. Encizo coolly shot the guy in the chest, and the Russian whirled and dropped to one knee, his mouth hanging open as pink froth foamed across his tongue.

Gasping from a punctured lung, the Soviet lunged to the radio and yanked open a metal clasp. Encizo saw the red button an instant before the Russian pressed it, and the Cuban ducked low and covered his head as the radio exploded, shredding the Russian's chest and face.

"*Cristo,*" Encizo rasped as he uncovered his head to examine the gory wreckage.

A salvo of full-auto slugs suddenly whined against the floor near the Cuban, and Encizo dived for shelter behind a pile of wooden crates. Bullets chewed into the boxes, and one projectile pierced the wood inches from the Cuban's left ear. He hissed through his teeth as a splinter stabbed the side of his neck.

Gary Manning located the sniper; armed with an AK, a Russian soldier positioned on the catwalk was doing his best to try to ice the Cuban warrior. Manning raised his Remington and aimed carefully. The shotgun boomed like a voice from the gates of hell as the weapon recoiled against the Canadian's shoulder.

A .50-caliber Sabot bullet rocketed from the Remington and crashed into the Soviet gunman's chest cavity, traveling upward to shatter his sternum and crush his heart and lungs. The impact hurled the Russian backward and he tumbled head over heels and sailed over the catwalk. The man didn't utter a sound as he dropped to the merciless concrete below.

David McCarter pulled the pin from a tear-gas canister and tossed it under the truck. The five men of Phoenix Force hastily donned their M-17 protective masks as a pungent green cloud filled the warehouse. Most of the Russians were either dead or unconscious, but two stumbled into the open, choking on gas, their hands clamped to the tops of their heads in surrender.

One Russian commando groped his way to a canvas bag full of field gear and extracted a gas mask. Something whirled past his head and struck the wall behind him. The Russian glanced over his shoulder at the star-shaped metal object lodged in the wallboard.

"Give up or die," Rafael Encizo ordered as he approached with his MP-5 in his fists.

The Soviet paratrooper wiped his eyes with his left hand as he held the gas mask overhead. Encizo moved closer, watching the Russian through the bug-eye lenses of his M-17. Suddenly the Russian hurled the gas mask at Encizo's face. The Cuban ducked instinctively and his opponent lunged forward and swung a roundhouse kick.

The boot connected with Encizo's MP-5, kicking the H&K blaster from Encizo's hands. The Russian slashed a cross-body karate chop to the Cuban's chest, hitting him under the heart and knocking Encizo off-balance. The Soviet paratrooper was trained in sambo, a Russian martial art similar to jujitsu. He grabbed the Cuban's shirtfront and dropped backward, planning to plant a boot in Encizo's abdomen to send him head over heels in a circle throw.

But Encizo was familiar with the tactic. He stepped to the side and avoided the Russian's boot, brushing it away with a forearm. Then the Cuban dropped on top of his opponent and slammed a fist to the Soviet's face.

The Russian's hand snaked out and grabbed at Encizo's hair, tugging the straps to his M-17 mask. The Cuban warrior rammed the heel of his palm to his opponent's elbow to knock the Russian's arm aside and promptly hammered the bottom of his fist into the man's breastbone. The Soviet gasped, swallowing more tear gas in the process.

The commando was gagging on the nauseous fumes, and Encizo, determined to keep his advantage, pinned the Russian to the floor. He punched his opponent again and seized the Russian's hair by the forelock. Encizo pumped his arm, slamming the man's head against the concrete floor twice, and the paratrooper's body went limp. Encizo retrieved his H&K machine pistol and dragged the unconscious Russian by an ankle.

"Check the place out carefully," Katz ordered, his voice distorted by the filters of his M-17 mask. "Haul the survivors outside before they choke to death in here."

"Sure hope one of these blokes has some answers for us," McCarter commented as he dragged an unconscious Russian toward the door.

"Yeah," Manning agreed, pushing two coughing survivors over

the threshold with the muzzle of his shotgun. "Otherwise we're back to square one and the KGB still has the dice for the next roll."

14

There had beeen thirty-four Russian agents inside the warehouse. Agent Connors and the other CIA and NSA operatives were astonished when they saw what sort of odds Phoenix Force had taken on without any of their men receiving more than a minor scratch or a slight bruise. Most of the Soviet agents did not survive the battle, and only eleven troops were still alive.

Calvin James, the unit medic, treated the wounded Russians while McCarter and Encizo stood guard over the Soviet prisoners. One of the KGB agents bit down on a plastic molar, bursting a cyanide capsule. His body convulsed violently for several seconds and then slumped lifeless among his comrades.

"Shit," James rasped. "The fuckers have suicide pills!"

"I'll take care of that," Katz announced, grabbing the closest Russian by the hair and jamming his trident hook into the man's mouth. "They can't bite my fingers unless they want some broken teeth."

The Israeli probed the lower molars, aware that the suicide capsules would be among the back teeth. He felt the smooth pearl quality of enameled plastic and clamped his hooks around the false tooth. Katz yanked the artificial molar from the Russian's mouth. The Soviet howled with pain as blood filled the gap in his gums.

"Sorry," Katz said. "The dentists at Red Square made this necessary."

Another Russian tried to bite his cyanide capsule before Katz could go fishing. James saw the man's face contort and quickly slammed a fist to the Soviet's jaw. The agent's mouth popped open and James smashed the side of his hand to the man's neck muscle to knock him unconscious.

"These guys are gonna make this a pain in the ass for us," James muttered sourly.

"Like pulling teeth," Katz agreed, moving to another Russian and pushing his prosthesis between the man's lips.

After all the suicide capsules had been yanked from the mouths of the remaining Soviets, James gave each man an injection of Thorazine to make certain none of them awoke for a couple of hours. The more fortunate Russians had slept through Katz's oral surgery and James gave these individuals a smaller dose of Thorazine to be certain he did not put them in a comatose state.

The senseless Soviets were loaded into vehicles to be transported to a safehouse on the outskirts of Houston. The safehouse was literally a house, a two-story dwelling with a basement and a two-car garage. The NSA had rented the place years ago and used it as a base for field agents on assignment in the Houston area. Unlike the CIA, the NSA has no restrictions concerning operations within the United States. Yet, unlike the FBI and the Justice Department, the NSA is able to conduct business abroad, as well. Nonetheless, the National Security Agency has endured little criticism compared to other American intelligence organizations, thanks largely to the fact that the NSA is lesser known that the others.

Dashiell McQueen and Sidney Nazarov were waiting at the safehouse when Phoenix Force and the other agents arrived with their Soviet prisoners. Both the NSA and CIA case officers were surprised by the number of Russians Phoenix had taken captive. When they heard how many Soviets had been inside the warehouse when the elite commando unit raided the place, McQueen and Dashiell were dumbfounded.

"The five of you took on thirty-four Russian agents?" McQueen asked with amazement. "How did you do it?"

"We surrounded them," Gary Manning answered.

"The raid could have gone better," Rafael Encizo remarked sadly. "The Soviets had a radio in the warehouse and they managed to call out before we could stop them. I tried to save the radio, but a Russian fanatic managed to destroy it. Of course, if I had been in his position I would have done the same thing, so I guess I shouldn't call him a fanatic."

"Maybe you should just admit you're one, too," David McCarter suggested with a wry grin.

"Look who's talking," Encizo said with a laugh. "You're such a mad dog we have to change your flea collar every ninety days."

"But I never claimed I'm *not* a fanatic," the Briton replied cheerfully.

McQueen and Nazarov exchanged nervous glances, uncertain of how safe it was to be in the same room with the five fearsome war machines...especially McCarter, whom they regarded as a homicidal maniac. The other members of Phoenix Force were accustomed to the Briton's bizarre sense of humor and took his odd comments in stride. Although even they were never sure when McCarter was kidding.

"We'll just have to forget about the radio," Katz said with a shrug. "Right now, we'll have to concentrate on questioning the people we captured. That's a task for Mr. Baker to handle."

"Oh?" James repied. "Is my name Baker this week? Must be. I'll need your help, Mr. Goldberg. I don't understand Russian, and the question-and-answer session will have to be in that language."

"Of course." Katz nodded.

"I speak Russian, too," Nazarov reminded them. "With ten enemy agents to question, it would save time if I helped."

"Thanks for the offer," Katz assured him. "But we can't be certain what the Soviets will talk about under the influence of scopolamine. It might be something that isn't classified for the CIA or NSA."

"For your eyes only, eh?" McQueen said with annoyance.

"Our *ears* only in this case," Encizo replied.

"Did you guys get the polygraph I asked for?" Calvin James inquired, opening a black medical bag to remove a set of syringes.

"Yeah," McQueen answered. "But what do you need a lie detector for? If you've got truth serum, that's better than a polygraph. Those machines can be outwitted by somebody trained to beat the detector."

"A polygraph registers heartbeat, blood pressure and stress level," James explained. "I want to be able to keep track of how the scopolamine affects each patient."

"Patient?" McQueen raised his eyebrows.

"That's right, man," the black warrior replied sharply. "And I don't intend to lose a patient due to carelessness. Scopolamine is a powerful drug. I don't want to kill one of those guys because his heart can't take the stress. Besides, some people can still manage to lie even under the influence of the drug. The polygraph can help us find out if we have a master liar on our hands."

"Then let's get to work," Katz suggested.

James and Katz questioned the Russians one by one. The interrogations lasted until dawn. The other members of Phoenix Force took turns guarding the prisoners and napping for three hours. The NSA and CIA agents were clearly upset at being excluded from the interrogations, and the fact that Encizo had found two spike microphones in the walls of the interrogation room did not improve the intel operatives' attitudes.

"I'm going to check outside from time to time," Encizo warned as he smashed the spike mikes in front of McQueen. "If I find the Warlock or some other agency snoop hanging around with a rifle microphone, I'll shoot the son of a bitch."

"Okay." McQueen sighed. "I'll tell them to leave."

"Tell them quick," the Cuban warned. "I'm going for a walk in about five minutes, fella."

James and Katz recorded their sessions with the Soviet captives, putting the replies on tape. It could be dangerous to have their own voices registered. It was unlikely anyone would be able to learn their true identities via a voiceprint, but it was also unwise to leave such things to chance.

The main reason the NSA and the CIA had been excluded from the questioning was because one of the Russians might mention a member of Phoenix Force by name, especially Gary Manning or Yakov Katzenelenbogen. Besides, circumstances might require the Stony Man commando team to take action without knowledge of any federal agencies. Phoenix might have to take immediate action without approval from Brognola and Stony Man. They had done so in the past, much to the dismay of the President of the United States, who did not like the most supersecret assault force attached to his office taking on unauthorized missions.

After hours of questioning Russians pumped full of truth serum, Katz and James learned that only one KGB operative even knew the Soviets were hunting a Canadian, a man with one hand, a Hispanic believed to be of Mexican descent, a tall black man and a fox-faced Caucasian who might be British, Canadian, American or Australian. None of the captives knew any names, and the Russian commandos did not even know what their mission was except to "crush enemies of the Soviet people."

"Jesus," Calvin James muttered. "How can these guys carry out a mission? They don't know anything."

"The Soviets don't tell their intelligence people any more than they absolutely have to," Katz explained. "That's how one keeps secrets. Don't tell anybody all the facts."

"I don't see how these dudes can function, man," James stated.

"Secrecy is both a strength and a weakness of the Soviet Union," the Israeli told him. "The USSR is controlled by a small ruling elite and they try to keep information, as well as power, in the hands of the few. A Russian platoon leader only has three or four sections under his command. That's all he's been trained to handle. Russian soldiers aren't taught to take over command if their officers are killed in battle. They're taught to take orders and carry out specified functions. The government is extremely paranoid. This attitude is evident in how they conduct intelligence and military operations. Field operatives are usually ignorant about what the mission is really about."

"You told me once before that intelligence agents are usually working in the dark," James remarked. "But isn't this a little extreme? These dudes hardly know what we look like."

"The KGB and the GRU are extreme examples," Katz agreed. "And as for knowing what we look like, that's all the combat soldiers need to know. Fortunately for us, they don't know much. Obviously, the only cover that has been blown is Gary's. The KGB might suspect me, but they aren't even close to finding out who you are. They're barking up the wrong tree concerning Rafael and they can't even pinpoint McCarter's nationality. We could be in worse shape, my friend."

"Could be better, too," James muttered. "Well, I guess we did learn a few things of value from these dudes. Want to share it with the others?"

"Why not?" the Israeli said with a shrug.

Katz and James joined the others and discussed what they learned from the interrogations. It did not take very long.

"We didn't have to edit these tapes, gentlemen," Katz announced, handing the cassettes to McQueen and Nazarov. He gave five to each man to avoid showing favoritism toward either CIA or NSA. "You're getting the replies to our questions just as the Soviet agents made them."

"So they must not have said anything very important," McQueen said with disappointment.

"There are some worthwhile statements," the Phoenix Force commander explained. "The Russian commandos didn't have much information for us except that two of them participated in the raid on Heinz Muller's survivalist camp in Georgia. Nine Soviets were killed in that battle, by the way. Some of Muller's men put up quite a fight. The paratrooper commander, Major Shalnev, personally killed Muller in hand-to-hand combat. His men were pretty impressed by this. Muller was a tough character and he had a knife prosthesis at the end of his arm. Major Shalnev is no pushover. Everybody make a mental note of that.''

''Is Shalnev KBG?'' McQueen inquired.

''He just said the major is a paratrooper,'' Nazarov snorted. ''Pay attention, Queenie.''

''Shalnev is an army officer,'' Katz said quickly, trying to prevent more infighting among the agents. ''But the KGB is running the show. All the paratroopers at the warehouse had been placed under command of the KGB agents in the group.''

''Is Colonel Burov in charge of the outfit?'' Nazarov asked.

''The paratroopers are working in the dark,'' Calvin James stated. ''But the KGB agents we questioned are aware they're working for a KGB colonel who is using a British passport. They only knew him as 'the colonel,' but I'd say there's little doubt that Burov is in charge.''

''So let's pick up Burov and his roommate and question them,'' Rafael Encizo suggested.

''Hold on,'' Katz urged. ''According to the men we questioned, there are still a lot of Russian troops and KGB agents we haven't accounted for yet. Major Shalnev, the commando leader, and Major Potapov, the GRU officer Nazarov identified from NSA photographs, are traveling in separate trucks somewhere in Texas. The exact number of enemy forces varies depending on whether one listens to the paratroopers or the KGB, but there is good reason to believe there are more than a hundred Soviet operatives out there somewhere.''

''A hundred?'' McQueen whistled softly. ''My God, that's incredible.''

''I've never heard of the KGB launching such a large military operation within the United States,'' Nazarav added.

"You five guys must have really done something to piss them off bad."

"We tried," McCarter replied proudly, apparently unconcerned by the odds they faced.

"I still think we should get our hands on Burov and pump the bastard full of truth serum," Encizo insisted.

"If we capture Burov and make him talk it still won't solve our problem," Katz explained. "The other Soviets will simply lie low and wait for another KGB commander to take Burov's place."

"Not if we can find out where they are and move in fast enough," the Cuban stated.

"You want to attack a hundred trained Russian agents?" McQueen asked with astonishment.

"Rather attack them than wait for them to come after me," Encizo answered. "And that's our only other choice."

"Trouble is we might not be able to break Burov fast enough," James commented. "One of the KGB dudes we interrogated did nothing but lie even under the influence of scopolamine."

"Are you sure?" Nazarov asked.

"The polygraph needle bounced every time that guy opened his mouth," James said. "He lied about his name, nationality, reason for being in the United States and involvement in espionage. I'll tell you, those dudes are trained inside and out. The subconscious has been conditioned as well as the conscious. If Burov is trained that well, I wouldn't count on him telling us shit. Probably have to use scopolamine two or three times in order to break him down...and that would probably kill him."

"Speaking of killing," McQueen inquired, "is that what you plan to do with the Russian captives? Terminate with extreme prejudice?"

"Despite what you might think, McQueen," Katz began dryly, "we're not murderers. You have the tapes and ample evidence to prove these men are Soviet agents operating within the United States. The National Security Agency and the Central Intelligence Agency can take care of them now.

Of course, the tapes aren't admissible in court, but there won't be a public trial, correct?''

"Of course not," McQueen said gruffly.

"What about that business at Muller's survivalist camp?" Calvin James asked. "The Russians tried to make that look like a bunch of militant blacks went on a murder spree and butchered everybody in the place. Some of the people who were killed were civilians who only wanted to learn how to take care of themselves. Everybody agrees this might spark a violent racial incident and a lot of innocent people, black and white, could get hurt."

"What do you expect us to do about that?" McQueen asked.

"How about trying to stop it from happening, asshole?" James snapped. "I thought that was our job, protecting the innocent from getting chewed up by the wolves?"

"Do you want to explain this or should I?" Katz asked the NSA agent.

"You're such a know-it-all, Goldberg," McQueen replied. "You do it."

The phone rang, and McQueen gratefully left the room to answer it while Katzenelenbogen turned to his young black partner and sighed.

"What do you think would happen if the American public learned that a unit of Russian soldiers commanded by the KGB managed to enter the United States and launch an attack on a privately owned paramilitary camp?" the Israeli inquired. "That this killer squad had slaughtered individuals whom you yourself described as civilians?"

"Guess most folks would figure our national security sucks," James replied.

"They'd be right," McCarter muttered grimly.

"That's beside the point, Masters," Katz declared. "The fact is people wouldn't feel safe in their own homes. They would think that this system of government is unable to protect them from foreign invaders."

"The bloody KGB entered the country through the UN and the Soviet embassy," McCarter stated. "And they were allowed to run all over the country. This isn't a new story, mate. They've been doing this sort of thing for years and they'll continue to do it as long as the Western nations fail to impose some restrictions on the bastards instead of giving them carte blanche to conduct espionage and subversion."

"That's true," Katz agreed. "But this particular incident was an organized military action by Soviet troops. It might very well be considered an act of war by the USSR against the United States of America. Now, if that became public knowledge it could lead to World War Three. Does anyone in this room want to take that risk?"

"Christ," James muttered. "Sometimes this job isn't so simple."

"That's because the world isn't so simple anymore, my friend," Katz said, placing his hand on the black man's shoulder. "Everything isn't black and white. A lot of it is gray and some shades are darker than others."

"I just got a call from Kovaks," McQueen announced as he rushed into the room. "Burov and the Russkie with him left the Hilton and managed to slip past all our surveillance people. The bastards left a tape recorder playing the sound of a typewriter clicking away. Damn thing was set right by the limpet mike we installed in the wall. They knew about the bug all along. God knows how long they've been gone or where they are now."

"Well," Encizo said with a sigh, "so much for my idea about grabbing the son of a bitch and forcing him to talk. Looks like we're back to square one after all."

"Maybe not," Gary Manning announced, breaking a long, thoughtful silence. "It's still our move, gentlemen."

"That sounds great," the Cuban said sadly. "But who do we move against and how do we do it?"

"We try to goad the KGB into making a move into our hands," the Canadian answerd.

"Wait a minute," McQueen began. "We can't have an all-out war in the streets of downtown Houston...."

"Nobody wants that," Manning replied. "You don't, we don't and neither do the Russians. So let's pick the next battleground and convince the KGB to meet us on our terms."

"Whatever you've got planned sounds wonderful," Katz commented. "I just hope it works."

"So do I," Manning admitted.

15

Colonel Vladimir Burov sat beside his aide, Captain Georgri Myshko as the junior officer drove a rented Volkswagen Rabbit to a small roadside motel between Houston and Huntsville. The two KGB officers entered the motel and signed the register as John Carlson and Richard Smith. They claimed to be cosmetic salesmen for a New York firm that was planning to open an office in the Houston area. The toothless old Texan behind the desk figured they were probably a pair of "gawd-damn homosexuals," but he rented a room to them anyway.

Burov and Myshko carried their suitcases to Room 14 and locked themselves in. Ten minutes passed before a knock at the door drew their attention. Both men approached with Makarov autoloaders held ready.

"Who is it?" Burov asked, his English accented with a well-schooled Cambridge flavor.

"Karl Marx," a familiar voice replied.

"Idiot," Burov growled as he yanked open the door. "That isn't funny."

"Perhaps my timing is off," Major Potapov remarked dryly as he stepped across the threshold. "I trust you cleverly avoided detection by the dreaded American spies of the imperialistic capitalist state?"

"We managed," Burov replied. He had no intention of telling the GRU officer that his room at the Hilton had been bugged. The colonel shut the door. "Are you certain you haven't been under surveillance, Major Potapov?"

"I'm certain," the GRU man assured him. "Major Shalnev is with the men in one truck and your KGB agent, Boris Shatrov, is with the other troops in the third vehicle. I assume you know what happened to the first truck to enter Houston?"

"We got the radio message the same time you did, Major," Burov said sharply. "Obviously the CIA or the FBI suspected the truck carrying the men under Comrade Antoli Metkov's command."

"They said they were under attack," Potapov said, recalling the radio message. "Since we didn't hear from them again, we'll assume they were wiped out or taken captive."

"Some may have escaped," Myshko suggested as he opened a case to remove a bottle of vodka. "Would you care for a drink, comrades?"

"Ah." Potapov smiled. "There is some welcome news after all. I would indeed like a drink. Then I think we should discuss how the hell we're going to get out of America and back to the Soviet Union."

"What are you talking about, you fool?" Burov snapped. "We haven't accomplished our mission."

"The mission is a failure, Comrade Colonel," Potapov said with a shrug. "It's painfully obvious. We've lost more than sixty men since we started this absurd manhunt for these mysterious commandos. Shatrov failed to capture or kill Manning and we haven't been able to locate the Canadian since he fled his cabin in Saskatchewan. The raid on Muller's camp was a total waste of time, to say nothing of human life. And now—"

"I don't need you to remind me that this mission has not met with success, Comrade Major," Burov said sharply. "But we must continue."

"Colonel," Potapov began, glaring at the KGB officer. "The morale among the men is very bad. They're beginning to regard us, you and I, as the enemy. I wouldn't be surprised if some of them decide to defect if we stay in this country much longer."

"Anyone who tries to defect is a traitor and shall be shot immediately!" Burov snapped. "That is a direct order, Comrade."

"Fine," Potapov said, rolling his eyes toward the ceiling. "As if enough Russian lives haven't already been lost, let's start shooting each other, too, eh?"

"Are you refusing a direct order from a superior officer?" Colonel Burov demanded. He glanced over his shoulder to glare at Myshko who had turned on the small black-and-white television set in the corner of the room. "What are you doing, damn it? This is no time to watch that idiot form of entertainment."

"I'm trying to find a news broadcast, Comrade Colonel," the KGB captain explained, turning the dial on the TV. "There may be a report concerning the incident at the warehouse last night."

"American television is full of lies," Burov spat.

"We should still hear what they're saying about the incident," Potapov stated, agreeing with Myshko.

"I think this is about the attack," Captain Myshko informed them, stepping away from the television to allow Burov and Potapov a clear view of the screen.

Film footage of the interior of a warehouse appeared. The place had been riddled with bullets and a wall was bashed in by the force of an explosion. The truck in the center of the bay area had been scarred by bullets. The windows of the cab had been shattered and the rear of the trailer was streaked with blood.

"The grisly aftermath of last night's shooting is one of the worst incidents of violence in Houston history," a square-faced reporter announced into a microphone as he stood outside the warehouse. "And the police appear to have no idea why this terrible carnage occurred. With me is Lieutenant Harlon Gibbs of the homicide division. Lieutenant, what statement have you got for the people of Houston at this time?"

"Well," the rawboned Texan cop began as he chewed a toothpick and cautiously watched the camera from the corner of his eye. "What we got here isn't just a multiple shootin'. I mean, it ain't as if somebody charged into this building and gunned down a bunch of businessmen or somethin'. It was a firefight. Ain't seen nothin' like it since I was in Nam. Tell you somethin' else, the fellers what got killed were armed with automatic rifles and submachine guns. Walt, hand me one of those Commie guns."

"Here you go," Walt, another cop, replied as he gave Gibbs an automatic rifle wrapped in plastic to preserve fingerprints. Walt smiled slyly at the camera before he stepped away.

"Okay," the lieutenant began, holding the rifle in front of the camera. "Now this gun is somethin' like the AK-47 rifles the Vietcong and the NVA used in Nam. There's writin' on this thing. I can't read it 'cause it ain't in English or Spanish, but I bet it's Russian or somethin' like that. Some of the weapons are American-made, but a lot of 'em look like they're from Moscow."

"What do you think that means, Lieutenant?" the reporter asked.

"Probably means the people here were either gunrunners or some kind of terrorists," Gibbs answered. "Didn't find any identification on the bodies, but we'll fingerprint 'em and check with the FBI. Can't know for sure, but I figure these boys probably got in some sort of argument and killed each other. Important thing is, folks don't have no call to get excited."

"I hope you're right, Lieutenant," the reporter said, glancing over his shoulder at a muscular figure who slipped through the roped-off area the police had constructed to keep a crowd of rubberneckers back.

"Will you get back, fella?" Gibbs snapped. "This is a restricted area."

"I'm just having a little look, officer," the man said in a loud clear voice.

"Shut your mouth and get behind that barrier, boy!" Gibbs said sharply. "Won't tell you again, neither."

"That's Gary Manning!" Colonel Burov exclaimed, pointing at the burly figure who meekly returned to the crowd. "The son of a pig has returned to the scene of the crime!"

"My God," Potapov said with amazement. "I think you're right, Colonel. That *is* Manning, and he's flaunting himself in front of the television camera as if he *wants* to be seen."

"Perhaps he suspects we'll see this broadcast," Myshko mused.

"Of course he does," Burov said, ignoring the TV reporter who concluded his story with some grim comment on the horrors of modern American society. "Manning's making an ass of himself on camera in order to deliver a message directly to us. He's telling us he and his gangster comrades slaughtered our people last night. He's thumbing his nose at us."

"More than that, Colonel," Potapov added. "Manning is letting us know he's still in the Houston area. He's daring us to come after him. Daring us to take on his special commando squad."

"He's trying to lure us into a trap," Myshko said grimly.

"*Da,*" Burov agreed. "Of course that's what they're doing, but we can't ignore such an opportunity."

"An opportunity to do what?" Potapov demanded. "To get more of our men killed?"

"Your defeatism and cowardly remarks are beginning to irritate me, Comrade Major," Burov said in a harsh, cold voice. "Are you suggesting that these American gangsters are too much for us to deal with?"

"I'm simply accepting the fact that we're dealing with very clever and dangerous adversaries, Colonel," the GRU officer answered. "I'm aware that you regard everyone born outside Moscow to be inferior and anyone who isn't a Russian to be a subhuman monkey, but arrogance and bigotry can make one careless. We can't afford to make mistakes, Colonel. And I believe playing into the enemy's hands would be a terrible mistake."

"Major," Burov began grimly, "we don't have any choice. We cannot return to the Soviet Union until we complete this mission. In case you fail to understand the situation, let me explain. You and I are the officers in charge of this mission. If the mission fails, we will be blamed. That means you and I will be executed or shipped off to a Siberian labor camp. If our superiors feel vindictive, they may also treat Major Shalnev in the same manner. We are fighting for our very survival, Major. We must complete this mission."

"Comrade Colonel," Captain Myshko began, "we have intelligence sources in the city of Houston, both informers who are willingly working for the KGB and people who serve us without their knowledge. Perhaps they can locate Manning."

"If he wants to be found," Burov said. "And apparently he wants us to find him."

"I suggest we attempt to locate Manning and then station a surveillance team to follow his actions for at least twenty-four hours," Potapov advised.

"That seems logical," Burov agreed. "That will give us enough time to trace his movements and plan our next move. Let me tell you one thing, Comrades, the next round will be a victory for us."

16

Gary Manning had rented a room at the Harmond Hotel on Clay Street. The KGB had little trouble learning this because Manning had signed for the room using his own name and paid for it with a charge card also in his real name. The Canadian made it very easy for the KGB informers to track him down.

It was too easy.

Colonel Burov personally supervised the surveillance of Manning's hotel room. The KGB were also adept at rifle microphones and spike mikes. The former were ruled out because they would tend to pick up worthless conversations from other tenants due to sound vibrations carried by the walls. Two spike mikes were implanted in the ceiling through the floor of the room above Manning's. Burov also ordered his snoops to tap Manning's phone and train a heat-detector on the Canadian's hotel room.

The latter device was similar to the heat-sensor mechanism of a guided missile, but far more sensitive. It was less complex than the missile's tracking device, but operated on the same principle. The surveillance detector was designed to register heat in a confined area and could be trained on a single section of a house or building. It would register body heat and even constructed an outline of the individual's body on a screen similar to a radar scope.

The first night of surveillance revealed little of interest. The form of a man in a prone position appeared on the screen. Burov was fascinated by the multicolored rainbow that danced across the shape.

"What do these colors mean?" the KGB colonel asked Captain Renkov, the surveillance expert.

"Different parts of the human body register different amounts of heat," Renkov explained. "The crimson hue is at the center of Manning's heart and also marks certain arteries where blood supply is noteworthy. The blue shades are warm, but not as warm as the red or green areas."

"What do you think he's doing?" Burov inquired.

"It appears he's asleep, Comrade Colonel," Renkov answered.

"Incredible," Burov shook his head. "The man knows we're stalking him and yet he sleeps like a child. What is that small white blob in the corner?"

"The heat from a television set, Comrade," Renkov answered. "There is a rather boring movie on the late show if you care to listen to the radio receiver picking up the spike mike transmissions. I'm not surprised it put Manning to sleep."

"I am," Burov stated. "What in blazes is that Canadian pig up to? None of this makes sense."

"We could move in right now and capture the bastard," Captain Shatrov, the Morkrie Dela officer declared. "I have a score to settle with Manning. He escaped from me in Canada, but I won't allow him to slip away again."

"Don't be an idiot, Captain," Burov said sharply. "This must be a trick. They're trying to lure us into a trap. We won't rush into this situation. We'll attack when it suits us and not until."

The night passed without event. However, the following morning at 0700 hours something quite remarkable occurred.

"Colonel!" Renkov said sharply, nudging his commander. "Colonel, wake up. Manning is gone!"

Burov had fallen asleep on a cot in the back of the Stallway Pianos Unlimited truck that housed Renkov and his detection gear. The KGB colonel sat up abruptly and glared at the surveillance man.

"What do you mean he's gone?" Burov demanded.

"He disappeared," Renkov answered. "One moment he was lying in bed and the next…he vanished."

Burov stared at the heat scope. All that remained on the screen was the white blob registering heat from the television set. Manning's body heat no longer appeared on the scope.

"Manning must have sneaked out when you were not watching," Burov growled, gathering up a transceiver.

"I swear, Comrade…" Renkov began.

Burov ignored him and transmitted to the other members of the surveillance unit who were positioned inside the hotel and at strategic points surrounding the building. "All eyes," Burov spoke into the mouthpiece. "Any sign of subject?"

"No sign," replied the voice of an agent stationed on the roof of a nearby building with a telescope trained on the hotel window to Manning's room.

"No sign," another spy replied.

"Has subject left premises, Control?" a third voice inquired.

Burov recognized the speaker. The voice belonged to Captain Igor Vitosho, the Bulgarian who had served under Colonel Kostov in Greece. Vitosho was bitter and vengeful. The Bulgarian wanted blood. Burov did not trust Vitosho and feared he might be unstable if a confrontation with his old enemies occurred.

"Don't ask questions," Burov told the Bulgarian. "Just answer the one I asked."

"No sign, sir," Vitosho said glumly.

"This is impossible," Burov told Renkov. "Check your machine. Make certain it is working properly."

"I've already checked it, Comrade," the surveillance expert assured him. "Manning is not in the room. I don't know where he is or how he got out of there undetected, but no one is in there now."

"Perhaps we should search the room," Shatrov suggested. The Morkrie Dela assassin also had a personal stake in the mission.

"That's probably what our opponents expect us to do," Burov told Shatrov. "We'd be marching right into their trap. Continue surveillance here. I'm going to contact Major Potapov and try to find some other leads on Manning."

Hours crept by as Colonel Burov gradually exhausted every clandestine source available to the KGB in the state of Texas. No one seemed to know anything about Gary Manning or any of the other commandos Burov had been sent to America to destroy.

Then, at 2300 hours, Renkov contacted Burov with some remarkable news. Manning had apparently returned to his hotel room. The heat detector registered that the Canadian was once again lying in bed, probably asleep, with the television playing softly in his room.

"Is there any way your machine could be tricked or scrambled?" Burov asked the surveillance expert.

"Even if that was possible they couldn't simply switch off a man's body heat," Renkov replied, speaking into the mouthpiece of his transmitter. "The heat from the television hasn't changed all day, so it isn't a scrambling device. All I can think is some sort of trapdoor in the wall by the bed that Manning might have slipped through unnoticed."

"Unless the building was constructed by the CIA," Burov said, "that doesn't seem likely. However, I see no other answer. Tell Shatrov to raid Manning's room and the one next door. Capture or terminate any person in either room."

"Understood, Colonel," Renkov replied grimly.

Burov switched off transmission. Major Potapov shook his head sadly and reached for a glass of vodka and ice.

"I hope you made the right decision, Comrade Colonel," the GRU officer said with a sigh.

"What other choice do we have?" Burov demanded, glaring at the major. "If this is a trick, it might be simply to delay us. Every day we remain in Houston we take a greater risk the CIA, FBI or even the local police will find us. We can't remain much longer, Major. Time is running out for all of us."

"It may run out for some sooner than others, Colonel," Potapov said as he raised the drink to his lips.

CAPTAIN BORIS SHATROV and Captain Igor Vitosho were delighted that the time for action had finally arrived. However, both men were professionals and both had tangled with Phoenix Force before. They would not allow their eagerness to make them careless. Shatrov was KGB, so he was in command. The Morkrie Dela officer selected ten of the best Russian agents in his team to back him up when he entered the hotel.

Vitosho was a Bulgarian. Shatrov regarded him as a lower form of animal life. Less than a Ukranian, but better than an American or even a Czechoslovakian. Shatrov did not like putting Russian troops under the command of a mere Bulgarian, but there seemed to be no other way. Of course, Vitosho would not be put in charge of KGB or GRU agents. Shatrov gave the Bulgarian command of eight Russian soldiers and ordered the captain to remain outside and cover the street.

Shatrov left nothing to chance. He positioned men on the roof of the hotel, in the lobby downstairs and the alleys outside. He even had snipers across the street armed with infrared scopes on their rifles. Shatrov and his men did not use the hotel elevator. Such contraptions can be boobytrapped too easily. As they mounted the stairs, they took Stechin machine pistols from their attaché cases. The weapons were equipped with sound suppressors. The 9mm ammo was a special low-velocity cartridge that functioned best with silenced weapons, but the slugs were mercury-core bullets for ultimate destruction on impact.

Boris Shatrov was leaving nothing to chance this time.

The Morkrie Dela commander and his hit team reached the fifth floor and poured into the hallway. Agents moved to Room 32, the room signed to Manning. Two other agents headed for the room next-door. Lock picks were inserted into keyholes and expertly jimmied the tumbler bolts.

No one set foot in the hall except the KGB unit. No witnesses. Thus far, everything had gone perfectly. The locks were picked. The Russians stood clear of the doors as they kicked them open. Machine pistols were trained on the gap to the two rooms, ready to open fire.

Nothing happened. Inside both rooms was the usual furniture one would expect to find in a second-rate hotel. No one appeared to be waiting inside either room. Shatrov and four other agents entered Room 32. The lights were off, but the television illuminated the bed where a still figure lay, apparently undisturbed by the KGB's abrupt visit.

Shatrov gestured to one of his men to approach the figure on the bed. The agent reluctantly obeyed, aware that Shatrov did not care to take the risk himself. The Russian held his Stechin ready as he reached forward and yanked the blanket away.

"Shto eto?" the agent said in amazement, staring down at the plastic figure sprawled across the bed.

"It's a mannequin," Shatrov replied, moving closer to get a better look.

At the center of the dummy's chest was a battery-operated thermal unit. Wires extended to the plastic torso and limbs, no doubt to distribute heat throughout the mannequin. An antenna wobbled from the thermal pack. The unit was operated by radio control.

"This explains how Manning's body heat was switched on and off," Shatrov said grimly. "The bastard was never here to begin with. We've been tricked, damn it!"

"Unit Four," Renkov's voice announced from the transceiver on Shatrov's belt. "Unit Four, do you read me?"

"Da," Shatrov said angrily, not bothering with the radio. He knew Renkov would hear him through the spike mikes in the ceiling. "We've been tricked!"

"I heard you before," Renkov told him. "Get out of there. The enemy must have something planned. This is too elaborate for a joke, Captain."

"I wondered how long it would take you idiots to show up," the voice of Gary Manning announced.

The Russians gasped, startled by the unexpected voice. They turned toward the dresser, swinging their machine pistols toward the sound of the Canadian's voice. Their weapons pointed at a bulky combination radio and cassette tape recorder on the top of the cabinet.

"You guys have been trying to track me down," Manning's voice continued. "Well, I'm going to make it easy for you. There's a map in the top drawer. The mountain range in Montana is where we'll meet you. There's a big red X marking the spot. Something you can relate to."

"Capitalist scum," Shatrov muttered as he yanked open the drawer and found the map.

"You clowns killed a lot of people in Georgia," Manning's tape continued. "They weren't part of this private little war. We don't want more innocent people hurt. That's why we'll meet you in Montana. It's a remote area and we can blow you all to hell without disturbing anyone's afternoon nap."

"We'll see who gets blown to hell," Shatrov said grimly, shoving the map in his coat pocket.

"By the way," the Manning tape concluded. "Have any of you assholes ever seen a TV series called 'Mission Impossible'?"

Shatrov blinked with surprise, confused by the question. Then the tape recorder exploded.

The blast was a low-velocity explosion, designed to detonate shrapnel rather than demolish the room. Shards of metal punched into the faces and torsos of Boris Shatrov and one of his agents. Projectiles punctured eyeballs and pierced brain matter. Jagged missiles sliced through skin and muscle to burrow into chest cavities. Both men fell to the carpet, blood pouring from their mutilated, lifeless bodies.

17

"Quickly! Someone get the map!" Captain Renkov shouted into the mouthpiece of his transceiver.

"Captain Shatrov is dead," a KGB agent's voice replied from the transceiver.

"I assumed as much," Renkov snapped. "Get the damn map and get out of there!"

"Affirmative, Comrade," the voice replied.

"This is Unit Six," another man declared. Unit Six was a surveillance team positioned on a roof. "I just saw a man fitting the description of Gary Manning and two other men enter a Volkswagen bus on the corner of Crawford Street. One of the men is a tall black and the other could be Hispanic."

"Are they traveling on Clay Street or Crawford?" Captain Vitosho's voice demanded.

"Crawford," Unit Six answered.

"Vito...Unit Three," Renkov snapped. "Do not pursue suspects. Unit Three, do you read me?"

Captain Vitosho did not reply. He had switched off his radio and yanked the battery out. The hell with these KGB flunkies. Spies are only good for sneaking around and gathering, Vitosho thought. They have no stomach for fighting. Vitosho was not an espionage agent. He was a soldier, a paratrooper with the best elite fighting unit in Bulgaria. The Russians under his command were also soldiers. Together they would crush the American gangsters.

"*I'deet'eh za mnoy!*" Vitosho told his men. "Follow me! We shall hunt down the enemy and destroy them!"

The Bulgarian captain had the keys to a nondescript Chevy sedan, but it was not large enough for Vitosho and his eight Russian troops. He gazed at the row of cars and pickup trucks parked at the curb. A lanky man dressed in soiled denim and a straw Stetson emerged from a tavern near the Harmond Hotel. The man took a set of keys from his pocket as he approached a battered old Ford pickup.

Vitosho did not hesitate. He dashed forward, drawing a Makarov automatic from a shoulder holster inside his tan sports jacket. The cowboy turned sharply, startled by the tall muscular blond Viking who charged toward him. Then the Texan saw the gun.

"You gotta be shittin' me, boy," he remarked, raising his hands overhead almost casually. "All I got in my wallet is a disappointed moth."

"Give me keys to truck," Vitosho ordered in broken English.

The Texan frowned. He considered the odds. Four more men with guns jogged up behind Vitosho. The odds were too great.

"Here you go, son," the Texan announced, tossing the keys to Vitosho. "What the hell, I got insurance."

Vitosho and his men piled into the truck. Three Russian paratroopers jumped in the back while the Bulgarian and another Soviet soldier climbed into the cab. The Chevy sedan pulled away from the curb first and bolted onto the street, carrying the other four Russian troopers. Vitosho followed, stomping the gas pedal to race the truck.

"Hey, Tom," a fat man called out as he stepped from the tavern. "What's going' on out here?"

"Some fellers just stole my truck," the lanky Texan said with a shrug. "Reckon I'll call the cops and have a couple more beers."

The sedan and the Ford pickup roared onto Crawford Street. The Chevy straddled a yellow line and drove between two lanes, its horn blaring at cars on both sides. Drivers cursed and beeped out profanity with their horns as they pulled out of the way. One vehicle was not fast enough.

Vitosho tagged the Oldsmobile with the front fender of the pickup truck. The car skidded into the rear end of a Buick and both cars awkwardly hopped onto the sidewalk.

Traffic parted for the demolition vehicles driven by the Bulgarian and his Russian allies. The Chevy sedan and the Ford pickup bullied their way to a right-hand lane and shot onto Caroline Street, desperately trying to catch up with the Volkswagen bus two blocks ahead.

David McCarter glanced in the side mirror at the driver's window as he steered the VW, then the British commando snapped open a valise on the seat beside him and patted the blue steel frame of his Ingram M-10.

"Company coming up behind us, mates," the Briton informed the other four members of Phoenix Force.

"We noticed," Encizo called from the rear of the Volkswagen as he worked the bolt to his H&K MP-5 machine pistol.

"I didn't figure the KGB would be this reckless," Calvin James added, feeding a 40mm cartridge grenade into the breach of the M-203 launcher attached to the barrel of his M-16 assault rifle.

"A high-speed chase through the streets of Houston is certainly sorry tactics for a clandestine organization," Yakov Katzenelenbogen remarked. The Israeli sat in the front seat with McCarter, an Uzi submachine gun in his lap.

"Maybe we should write a letter of complaint to the Kremlin," James commented dryly.

"I didn't think they'd be crazy enough to try to chase us," Gary Manning said as he unfolded the metal stock of his Remington shotgun. "But I'm sure glad we prepared for something like this just in case."

"I just hope these guys don't have anything planned that wasn't included in our script," Encizo remarked.

The wail of a siren shrieked through the night. A police car was speeding up behind the enemy pickup truck, its warning lights flashing. A second cop cruiser was following the lead squad car. Vitosho shouted an order to the soldiers in the back of the truck. The Russians reluctantly obeyed, and two men opened fire with Soviet PPS submachine guns.

Steel-jacketed 7.62mm projectiles smashed through the windshield of the first police car and bullets tore into the faces and chests of the two cops in the front seat. The officer at the wheel slumped to the side, turning the steering wheel abruptly to the right. The squad car swung into a Dodge Dart parked at the curb. Metal crunched and the crumpled hood of the cruiser popped open. The cops inside were sprawled across the seat. The backrest was streaked with blood and stuffing leaked from bullet-punctured upholstery.

The second squad car quickly swung into the next lane and hopped onto the sidewalk, nose-diving onto a bench next to a bus stop. Fortunately the bench was not occupied at the time. The cops realized trying to pursue the fleeing pickup truck would be suicide, and hastily radioed headquarters for backup.

"Jesus," James rasped. "They burned those cops, man. These fuckers are nuts. They don't give a diddly-shit about innocent bystanders."

"We've got to get this war off the streets," Encizo added.

"I'm trying," McCarter snapped, steering the Volkswagen onto Prairie Street.

The Phoenix Force vehicle shot under the I-45 overpass and continued to head northwest. The enemy Chevy and Ford pickup followed, closing the distance quickly. Then Phoenix Force saw something they had hoped to avoid.

Four squad cars formed a barricade at the intersection of Prairie and Houston. Cops armed with pump shotguns were braced behind the vehicles. An officer with a bullhorn ordered the Volkswagen to halt.

Of course, Phoenix Force could not oblige, but they did not intend to shoot police officers, either. Manning and Encizo pulled the pins from two green canisters and lobbed the grenades out the windows. The canisters sailed into the center of the police blockade and the cops ducked low as billows of green smoke clouded the area.

McCarter stomped on the gas pedal. The VW crashed into the corner of a squad car, knocking the car aside. A headlight shattered, but the vehicle suffered little other damage. McCarter kept driving, speeding through the green fog and heading for the outskirts of Houston.

The Chevy sedan and Ford pickup also burst through the police blockade. Russian troops sprayed the cops with machine gun fire. Another Houston policeman fell, his chest pulverized by high-velocity slugs. Two other cops fired shotguns at the fleeing pickup and a Soviet gunman received a blast of buckshot in the upper torso. The impact hurled him from the back of the truck. Vitosho did not ease up on the gas pedal as the slain Russian's body tumbled across the pavement.

David McCarter steered the Volkswagen onto a dirt road and swung onto the narrow pathway of a construction site. Mounds of dirt and stacks of metal girders surrounded the steel skeleton of a building in progress. McCarter slowed as he moved the VW around a pile of loose earth. Rafael Encizo popped open the rear door and jumped, landing in the soft dirt and rolling aside as Calvin James followed his example and tumbled onto the soil.

As the Volkswagen drove toward the framework of the building, a lone figure dashed to a tiny glass-and-aluminum guard shack. The night watchman did not know what was going on, but he realized these invaders were better armed than he was and he was not paid enough to risk his life tangling with guys packing military hardware.

The Chevy sedan roared down the dirt road, followed by Vitosho in the pickup. As the Chevy closed in rapidly for the kill, Calvin James triggered his M-203 grenade launcher. A 40mm projectile full of high explosives smashed into the sedan and the grenade exploded, blasting the Chevy to pieces and tearing its driver and passengers apart. The gas tank blew, spewing flaming liquid across the debris. Burning wreckage littered the site as Captain Vitosho desperately turned the steering wheel to avoid driving straight into the flaming ruins.

Vitosho found himself lodged between two stacks of steel girders and quickly ducked when the end of a girder suddenly filled the windshield. The Russian seated next to him was not as fortunate. Glass shattered from the impact and the steel beam burst through, splattering the skull of the horrified Soviet trooper.

The violent collision jarred the Ford, and two of the soldiers in the back were thrown from the truck. The third dropped to the floor of the pickup and rose with his PPS subgun ready. He did not get a chance to use it. Calvin James fired his M-16 and three 5.56mm slugs burned through the Russian's face and popped open his skull like a ripe watermelon.

One of the men who had fallen from the back of the truck rose to one knee and aimed a Stechin machine pistol at James's position. The black warrior ducked behind a stack of girders as the Russian fired a burst of 9mm slugs. Bullets whined off metal and screamed into the night sky, but none of the projectiles struck James.

The Soviet gunman got one chance to burn a member of Phoenix Force and he blew it. He did not get another. Rafael Encizo, positioned behind another stack of girders, opened fire with his H&K machine pistol. A 9mm slug caught the Russian at the base of the neck. Vertebrae snapped and the spinal cord was severed. The Soviet triggerman fell on his face, his body barely able to twitch as death claimed it.

The other gunman who had been thrown from the pickup quickly rolled to the end of the nearest stack of girders. He had dropped his S&W M-76 subgun, but he still had a .38 caliber Ruger revolver. The Russian dragged the handgun from a holster at the small of his back and tried to determine where Encizo was hiding.

He did not notice Calvin James creep around the corner behind him. The black commando raised his M-16 and prepared to stamp the butt plate between the Russian's shoulder blades. Suddenly the Soviet turned, and James hammered the plastic stock of his assault rifle against his opponent's wrist, striking the .38 from the man's grasp.

The Russian paratrooper responded by charging the black man. His left hand seized the frame of the M-16 and he swung his right fist into James's face. The Phoenix pro's head bounced from the punch. The Soviet chopped the side of his hand across James's forearm and wrenched the rifle from his grasp.

James's right leg streaked out in a fast reverse round-house kick. The side of his foot slammed into the Russian's face, propelling the man back against the girders. James swung a left hook to his opponent's jaw and drove a fist to the Russian's breastbone. The Phoenix fighter grabbed the M-16 by the barrel and yanked it from the dazed Russian's hand.

With a deft stroke similar to that used with a broom while sweeping the floor, James whipped the hard plastic stock of the assault rifle between the Soviet soldier's legs. The Russian gasped in agony and clasped both hands to his genitals. The man's mouth hung open and his eyes rolled up, the pupils vanishing beneath eyelids. Then he sank to the ground and passed out.

"That's what happens when you fight dirty with a kid from Chicago, my man," James told his senseless opponent.

Captain Igor Vitosho crawled out of the Ford pickup truck. The Bulgarian officer was splattered with blood and brain matter from the decapitated corpse that had been seated next to him. He had been stunned and shaken by the crash, but had escaped uninjured. As Vitosho prepared to reach through the broken window to retrieve his Makarov, he heard a steely voice behind him.

"Freeze, Comrade," Rafael Encizo ordered as he appeared at the rear of the truck, his MP-5 aimed at the Bulgarian.

Vitosho turned. His eyes widened with surprise and rage when he recognized the Cuban commando. Vitosho's handsome Aryan face twisted into an ugly mask of hatred and fury.

"You," the Bulgarian hissed through clenched teeth.

"Captain Vitosho," Encizo said warmly. "Thought I saw you for the last time in Greece more than a year ago."

"I've waited for this moment," Vitosho announced, stripping off his soiled jacket. A bayonet rested in a scabbard clipped to his belt. "I've been waiting for another chance to kill you, Santos, or whatever your real name is."

"I already kicked your ass back in Greece," Encizo replied. "I could have killed you then."

"You should have, you little spic bastard," Vitosho said angrily.

"I can do it now," the Cuban replied, gesturing with the Heckler & Koch machine pistol. "I have the gun, Vitosho."

"Afraid to face me on fair terms?" The Bulgarian smiled smugly. "I've been training with a knife, spic. I won't make it so easy for you this time."

Vitosho drew the bayonet from its scabbard. Encizo's finger tightened around the trigger of his MP-5, but he did not fire the weapon. The Cuban sighed and pulled the Cold Steel Tanto from its belt sheath.

"So you're not a coward after all," Vitosho remarked.

"I should probably just shoot you through the kneecaps," the Cuban commented as he lowered the MP-5 and dropped it to the ground. "But I could never resist a challenge from a loudmouth."

Vitosho crouched in a knife-fighter stance, digging the toe of his right foot into the loose earth. Encizo adopted a similar position, his knife held low, free hand poised in a karate claw. The Bulgarian suddenly snapped a kick, hurling dirt from his boot upward into Encizo's face.

The Cuban staggered backward, blinking to try to work the dirt from his eyes. He didn't drop his guard, aware that Vitosho would make his move. As the Bulgarian executed a bayonet lunge, Encizo swung his Tanto. Blades clashed with a metallic ring. Vitosho suddenly pivoted and thrust his elbow in a high stroke, hitting Encizo on the point of the chin.

Encizo fell against the side of the Ford pickup. Lights popped painfully inside his head. Vitosho had indeed learned some new tricks since they first fought at Krio Island. The bayonet slashed at the Cuban's wrist, trying to sever veins and arteries to wound Encizo and disarm him the same time. The Phoenix commando jerked his arm out of the path of his opponent's blade and stepped to the left as he struck out with the Tanto. The ultrasharp Cold Steel edge sliced cloth and flesh to bite into the Bulgarian's deltoid muscle.

Vitosho gasped in pain and jumped back, blood oozing from his wounded shoulder. His right arm moved woodenly. He clenched his teeth as pain lanced through his damaged limb. Vitosho tossed the bayonet to his left hand and lashed out at Encizo's knife arm.

The Cuban danced out of reach. Vitosho swung a cross-body stroke, aiming his blade at the Phoenix pro's face, but Encizo ducked under the bayonet. As the long blade whistled overhead, Encizo slashed his Tanto across Vitosho's belly. The Bulgarian screamed as blood poured from a deep stomach cut.

Vitosho was as tough and determined as hell. His leg suddenly snaked out, slamming a hard sidekick to the Cuban's chest. Encizo was knocked off his feet. He fell and rolled backward, springing to his feet as the Bulgarian charged once more.

Encizo flipped the knife in his hand and grabbed it in an overhand grip, the blade jutting from the bottom of his fist. He allowed his opponent to close in and quickly swung a left-leg roundhouse kick. His boot struck Vitosho's wrist, kicking the bayonet from the Bulgarian's fingers. The Cuban pivoted with the motion of his kick and thrust the Tanto down, driving the steel point into Vitosho's abdomen.

Sharp steel stabbed deeply into the Bulgarian's stomach. Blood washed Encizo's wrist. The liquid was hot and thick, like scarlet soup. Encizo had felt this sensation many times before. He ignored the blood and released the Tanto, leaving the knife buried in his opponent's belly. He slashed the side of his hand across Vitosho's throat, and the karate chop crushed the Bulgarian's thyroid cartilage and closed off his windpipe. Captain Igor Vitosho toppled to the ground and died.

"Did you have to kill him, man?" Calvin James inquired as he appeared at the rear of the pickup truck.

The Cuban shrugged as he knelt beside Vitosho's corpse. As Encizo yanked the Tanto from lifeless flesh, the blade came free with an ugly sucking sound. "It sure seemed like a good idea at the time," he said.

18

Phoenix Force abandoned the Volkswagen near the construction site and piled into a Volvo station wagon that had been concealed behind a cluster of bushes as a backup vehicle. McCarter once again took the wheel.

"Where to, gents?" the Briton inquired cheerfully.

"Head north," Katz explained. "Get on I-45 and head back into Houston. The police will be expecting us to be leaving the city in a VW. By now the highway patrol will be on the alert and they'll have roadblocks outside the city. The safest thing for us to do is head right back where we came from."

"The NSA and the CIA won't be very happy with us," James remarked. "We caused another public incident."

"They'll be delighted when we tell them we're leaving Texas," Gary Manning assured him. "As far as they're concerned, this mission is over."

"So we fly via military bases from Texas to North Dakota and then what?" Encizo asked. "We'll get a helicopter large enough to carry all five of us and trust David to fly us to Montana?"

"Ye of little faith," McCarter snorted.

"That's the plan," Manning confirmed. "Then we'll just have to hope the KGB accepts our challenge and meets us on our ground."

"They will," Katz said. "They don't have any choice now. Colonel Burov can't return to the Soviet Union empty-handed, especially since he's lost so many men since this mission began."

"He might not want to lose any more," James comented.

"Burov will be willing to sacrifice the lives of all his men in order to save his own," Katz said sadly. "One doesn't become a colonel in the KGB without being very ruthless. Besides, putting one's life on the line is part of this business. Wouldn't all of us be willing to give up our lives rather than fail a mission?"

"I wouldn't be so casual about throwing away other people's lives," Manning commented. "Guess that's why we're the good guys and they're the bad guys."

"That depends on your point of view," Katz said with a shrug. "The Russian soldiers are following orders. The KGB sees us as a threat and the party in Moscow feels their 'world revolution' is a crusade rather like the concept of Manifest Destiny or Hitler's Third Reich. Everyone can justify his actions. That's part of human nature."

"You figure we have to justify what we're doing?" Encizo inquired.

"We're trying to stay alive," Katz replied. "I don't think that needs any justification."

COLONEL BUROV WAS FURIOUS. The American gangsters had tricked him, lured his men into a trap. Captain Shatrov and another KGB agent had been killed by that Canadian devil's booby-trapped tape recorder. To make matters worse, that Bulgarian idiot had rushed off to his slaughter and gotten eight good Russian soldiers killed, as well.

"The recorder bomb was quite clever," Potapov remarked as he sat on a bench in Tranquility Park and unwrapped a hot dog. "The enemy obviously had a hidden microphone of their own in the room. The recorder was radio operated to be certain no one could activate the device by accident."

"I'm so glad you admire those bastards," Burov hissed, kicking at a group of pigeons who were begging for bread crumbs. "They also killed more of our men, Comrade Major."

"I do not mean to praise our enemies, Colonel," the GRU major assured him. "But I respect professionalism, even when it is found on the other side. I also admire the fact these American 'gangsters,' as you choose to call them, are concerned with protecting the lives of innocent people."

"The lives of innocent *Americans*," Burov snorted. "That is a contradictory statement."

"All Americans can't be so terrible, Colonel," Potapov said with a shrug. "Don't forget they were our allies during the Second World War when we fought the Nazis. When Berlin fell, Russians and Americans were singing and dancing in the streets, side by side."

"That was forty years ago, Major," Burov stated. "We haven't been allies for a long time and we won't be in the foreseeable future."

"Our governments will see to that," the GRU officer commented dryly. "My point is, we're dealing with very skilled professionals. If we accept their challenge and go to that mountain range in Montana, we'll be heading into a trap."

"Of course it's a trap," Burov snapped. "But we'll—"

"I believe I've heard this speech before," Potapov said with a sigh. "You were very confident we could outfox these Americans at the hotel. You suspected a trap then and you thought you could outwit them. Almost half our men have been killed during this mission. We can't afford any more rash mistakes."

"I see." Burov smiled with all the warmth of a crack in a frozen headstone. "You do not approve of how I have handled this mission, Major. I suppose you intend to file a complaint with the General Staff when we return to Moscow."

"Of course not, Colonel," Potapov lied. "But I want to survive to return to the Soviet Union and I'd like to see the rest of us return, as well. So far your strategy has not worked, Comrade Colonel."

"If our mission is successful," Burov mused, "you won't have a leg to stand on, as they say in this country of swine. No one will listen to your complaints anyway, Colonel."

"No one will listen if I'm dead, either," Potapov stated. "I'm certain that thought has crossed your mind, Colonel."

"Don't be absurd," the KGB colonel said. "I wouldn't want you dead, Major. We are both officers in the Soviet Union and concerned with intelligence and espionage against the enemies of the Soviet state. Killing you would be like killing my own brother."

"Do you have a brother, Colonel?" Potapov inquired.

"He's dead," Burov replied. "But let's concentrate on the enemy, Major. I have a plan."

"I hope it includes the possibility that our enemies are going to try to lead us into an ambush," Potapov remarked. "And you'd better assume they'll have help. CIA, NSA, FBI or perhaps an entire division of American Special Forces or U.S. Marines might be waiting for us. After all, these people obviously have received assistance from other government organizations."

"I'm not so sure they'll do that," Burov said, "for a purely selfish reason. They're obviously keeping their identities secret from American intelligence networks or we would have more information about them. Indeed, the organization they work for must be top secret, as well. They won't want too many outsiders involved in this final showdown because it would jeopardize security. However, my plan will allow us to check conditions before we go into battle."

"I hope you're right, Colonel." Potapov sighed.

"Don't worry, Major." Burov smiled thinly. "If the gangsters try to lure us into an ambush by an army of enemy agents or soldiers, we'll call off the attack and strike at another time. However, if they're foolhardy enough to face us alone, the outcome of a battle between five men pitted against more than one hundred is rather easy to predict."

19

Gary Manning carefully placed the Claymore mine between two rocks. To be certain the Claymore was well camouflaged, the Canadian explosives expert shoveled out a small hole in front of the rocks and planted a red osier dogwood. The shrub was native to Montana and would not seem suspicious on the face of the mountain.

Satisfied with his work, Manning crept along the rock ridge to check on Rafael Encizo's progress. The Cuban member of Phoenix Force had placed a NATO C-1 machine gun under the trunk of a rotted whitebark pine. The tree had been struck by lightning and had fallen on its mangy branches, creating an arch. The dead pine was surrounded by a rather odd-looking wildflower called an Indian pipe, which resembled a mutated tulip. The combination created an ideal place for concealment.

Encizo had mounted the Canadian-made C-1 on a special revolving tripod. The swivel to the mount and the triggers at the back of the gun were linked to a battery-powered control unit with a radio receiver to activate via remote control. Encizo straightened his back and wiped the back of a hand across his brow.

Something moved among the rocks farther down the face of the mountain and Encizo's hand instinctively reached for the S&W M-59 on his hip. He did not draw the weapon, realizing the shape below was too small to be human. It was a ground squirrel, less than six inches long from tail to nose. The little rodent scrambled across the rock wall and slipped into a burrow. Encizo sighed with relief as Manning approached.

"Getting a little jumpy," the Cuban admitted. "I think I prefer it when we go after the enemy instead of waiting for them to find us."

"I'd rather be the hunter than the hunted, too," Manning agreed. "But hopefully we'll be able to reverse roles when the assault force arrives."

"It'll be more like an mutual open season," Encizo replied. "Everybody trying to kill everybody else."

"Wonder how long we'll have to wait," Calvin James remarked as he surefootedly climbed down the side of the mountain to join them on the ledge.

"Getting impatient, Cal?" Encizo inquired.

"Waiting for the enemy to show himself makes me nervous," the black commando confessed. "That was the tough part about Vietnam, man. You knew the Cong were out there somewhere in the jungle. You didn't know where and you didn't know how many, but they were going to hit at any moment. It was almost a relief when somebody started shooting at you after hours of waiting and wondering when it would happen."

"I remember," Manning told him with a firm nod. "Did you get the rope set up on the east cliff?"

"Yeah," James confirmed. "Complete with a surprise in place. Brings a whole new meaning to the term 'rope trick.'"

"What's McCarter up to?" Manning asked as he noticed the British warrior positioned farther down the rock wall, hammering wooden stakes into cracks among a cluster of boulders.

"He's working on a new booby trap," James explained. "Dave calls it a combination of the Malaysian mantrap, the punji stick and SAS dirty tricks rolled into one."

"I've got to see this," Encizo commented, shuffling along the rock ledge toward McCarter.

The Cuban had to scale the rock wall using hand and footholds to reach the Briton's position. McCarter was the best mountaineer of Phoenix Force and he did not mind working on steep surfaces where a slip would mean a bone-crushing three-hundred-foot tumble to the base of the mountain. Apparently McCarter had finished driving stakes into the boulder cracks. He drew a smatchet from a belt sheath and began chopping at the ends of the wooden poles.

A smatchet is something of a cross between a machete and a Roman short sword. It was a favorite weapon and tool of British commandos during World War II, but Encizo had never seen one outside a military museum before. McCarter wielded the big knife with ease, hacking chips from the stakes to form crude points. As Encizo drew closer, he saw McCarter had planted almost a dozen stakes among the boulders and in the ground surrounding the area.

"Hullo, mate," McCarter said cheerfully. "If you came to give me a hand, you can start sharpening the ends of the other stakes for me."

"What is this thing supposed to do?" Encizo asked. "It looks mean, nasty and vicious whatever it is."

"Mean, nasty and vicious is exactly what it is," the Briton assured him. "After all the stakes are nice and sharp, I'm going to cover up the area with some shrubs or brush."

"*Madre de Dios,*" Encizo rasped, glancing up the mountain at the machine gun he had planted by the rotted pine. "I think I understand now."

"I thought you'd appreciate it." McCarter grinned as he continued to hack away at the end of a stake.

"It's diabolical," the Cuban remarked.

"Thank you," McCarter replied. "I knew you'd approve."

By nightfall Phoenix Force had completed all preparations for the final confrontation with the KGB assault force. Manning built a campfire outside the cabin and the five men sat around the blaze, heating C rations on the hot stones encircling the fire. McCarter took a can of Coca-Cola from an ice chest and popped the top. Yakov Katzenelenbogen heated water in a canteen cup for tea while the others were content to drink coffee.

"I guess we're about as ready as we'll ever be," Encizo remarked as he spooned some stringy beefsteak from a can.

"I just wish you'd had something else stored in your cabin besides C rations, Gary," Calvin James muttered. "They make for a lousy last meal."

"Does anyone want to trade?" Katz inquired. "I've got pork and beans."

"Oh, sorry about that, Yakov," Manning said, rummaging through a crate of rations.

"Honest mistake," the Israeli said with a shrug.

"This can says it's chicken and dumplings," the Canadian announced, handing a new one to Katz.

"At least it sounds a bit more kosher," Katz said.

"It occurred to me that it might take the Russians quite a while to get to Montana," Encizo remarked. "We might have to wait a week or two."

"Shit," James muttered. "I hope it doesn't take that long. I'm already getting cabin fever and we've hardly spent any time in the cabin."

"The KGB has connections all over America," Katz stated. "They won't have much more trouble getting out of Texas than we had. They could be here tomorrow or they might let us sweat awhile and hit when they feel the time is right."

"I don't think they can afford to wait too long," McCarter commented, munching on some C ration pound cake. "They knew the NSA had Burov's hotel room bugged in Houston and they have to assume we've taken a few prisoners and interrogated them. The KGB must realize they can't carry out business in the U.S. on the same combat level they've been maintaining since this mission began. The heat is on and they've either got to hit and hit hard or take the chance of being burned up by a nationwide manhunt of the NSA, CIA, FBI, Justice Department and whoever else wants to join the bleeding posse."

"I think David's right," Manning agreed. "But I'm sure the KGB will try some recon before they launch an attack. They'll send some agents to scout the area first to make certain we don't have nine hundred guys waiting for them. They'll also want to get an idea of the terrain before they hit us, but when they hit us they're going to come after us with everything they've got."

"That makes it even," James mused. "Cause that's what we're going to do to them."

"But there are going to be a lot more of them than us," Encizo reminded the black warrior.

"So what's new?" James chuckled. "Fighting impossible odds is our specialty, man."

"This time is different for two reasons," Katz explained. "In the past, we've usually penetrated an opponent's defenses and had the element of surprise in our favor."

"We've arranged some surprises," McCarter stated.

Katz nodded. "But the advantage will still be with our assailants. The second point is the fact that most of our opponents will be Russian comandos, not KGB agents. Soviet elite fighting men have been vigorously trained for open combat. Their skills will be similar to our own. The only thing in our favor is experience and the fact we've been trained to act individually, as well as a team. Individualism isn't encouraged in the Soviet Union."

"Neither is imagination," Manning added. "And we've come up with some imaginative defenses here. I guess we'll find out if our bag of tricks is good enough when the Russians make their move."

"Wonder how they'll attack," James said, sipping his coffee.

"We can only guess," Katz declared. "But if we think how we would handle a raid if we were in the Russians' boots, then we'll have a good idea of what they'll probably do. Our enemies are professionals. That means they think like we do."

"Kind of like fighting ourselves," James remarked.

"Not quite," McCarter commented, pulling a burning stick from the campfire to light a Players cigarette. "There are only five of us."

20

Olsen's Choppers Unlimited was a small airfield located near Logan's Pass. The business was owned by Lawrence Olsen, a former Navy pilot who employed four other military veterans to jockey his three Bell HH-1K helicopters. Olsen also had two full-time mechanics who kept his whirlybirds in top condition.

Olsen's choppers were generally used for the tourist trade, transporting vacationers throughout Glacier National Park. On more than one occasion Olsen's copters had assisted the park rangers in rescuing stranded tourists who were lost within the million-plus acres of the second largest of the Rocky Mountain national parks.

Olsen leaned back in his chair and propped his feet up on the battered old desk that was scarred with cigarette burns and penknife doodles. He leafed through the June issue of *National Geographic*, daydreaming about places he had never been but hoped one day to visit.

The door opened and two men entered Olsen's tiny office. He was surprised because he had not heard a vehicle pull into the gravel driveway. One man was tall, well built and rugged. His companion was a bit overweight and slightly balding. The elder man smiled at Olsen and extended his hand as he approached the desk.

"Hello," Major Potapov greeted. "I'm Bob Swenson and this is George Fuller."

Major Shalnev simply nodded at Olsen.

"Howdy," Olsen replied, taking his feet off the desk and placing his magazine on the counter. "You fellas want to take a ride in a helicopter?"

"Yes, indeed," Potapov confirmed.

"Fine," Olsen said. "We'll—"

A scream suddenly erupted from outside. Olsen glanced at the faces of the two men. Neither stranger's expression registered surprise. Larry Olsen immediately reached for the top right-hand desk drawer. He yanked it open and prepared to grab his .357 Smith & Wesson revolver.

Major Shalnev leaped forward. He slapped his palms on the desk top as he vaulted over the piece of furniture feet-first. A boot slammed into Olsen's chest, knocking him back into a wall. The Russian paratrooper nimbly landed beside his opponent and slashed the side of his hand under Olsen's heart. Olsen gasped as the karate blow knocked the wind from his lungs, but he swung a right cross at Shalnev's face.

The Russian commando caught Olsen's arm at the wrist and elbow. He pivoted quickly, throwing the American off-balance. Olsen stumbled away from the wall. Fotapov tried to grab him, but Olsen lashed a fist to the GRU officer's face. The Russian staggered backward, stunned by the blow.

Olsen turned to confront Shalnev. The paratrooper's leg shot out and smashed a high sidekick to the American's face. Olsen fell heavily onto his back. Shalnev bent a knee and fell forward, landing on Olsen's breadbasket with all his weight. The American groaned, his mouth falling open in a silent scream. Shalnev chopped the edge of his hand across his opponent's neck muscle and rendered Larry Olsen unconscious.

"Are you hurt, Major?" Shalnev asked, turning to Potapov.

"Only my pride," the GRU agent replied, dabbing a finger to his split lip. He looked at the blood and clucked his tongue with disgust. "I certainly wasn't much help."

"The man is out of action," Shalnev stated. "And we did not have to kill him. That is all that matters. *Da?*"

"You're right, Major," Potapov agreed. "Too much innocent blood had been shed already. Unfortunately the KGB has never objected to killing a few civilians to accomplish a mission. And, as much as we wish otherwise, the KGB is in charge of this mission."

"It is unfortunate that innocent people must be harmed during war, Major," Shalnev stated. He agreed with what Potapov said, but he did not intend to admit it. Potapov was GRU and Soviet military intelligence was subservient to the KGB. Thus, Shalnev did not fully trust Major Potapov.

"You memorized that rhetoric very well, Major," Potapov said, laughing. "Save it for Colonel Burov. He likes to hear that shit. I don't."

"Let's just concentrate on finding the Americans we were sent to liquidate," the paratrooper urged. "My men are eager to return to Russia."

"There is no Russia, my friend," Potapov said with a sigh. "Only the Soviet state run by Communists. You already said you are not a party member, correct?"

"I will do my duty to my country, Major," Shalnev declared. "That is the only politics a soldier need concern himself with."

Colonel Burov entered the office, Makarov pistol in hand. He glanced down at the unconscious figure of Larry Olsen on the floor. The KGB officer nodded his approval.

"Is he dead?" Burov asked.

"There is no need to kill him," Potapov replied. "He knows nothing."

"Very well," Burov agreed. "Tie him up and gag him. The other Americans at this airfield have been taken care of, as well."

"Are they all dead?" Shalnev inquired stiffly.

"That doesn't really matter, Major," Burov insisted. "What matters is the fact that we now have three helicopters to use in our attack. Major Shalnev, I shall place you in command of the air strike. Arm the helicopters as best you can and take as many men as you can load into the aircraft without having them sit on each other's laps."

"And the rest of my men, Colonel?" Shalnev demanded.

"Nothing belongs to you, Major Shalnev," the KGB officer said sharply. "Least of all those Russian soldiers. They, like you, belong to the Soviet state. The soldiers will participate in a ground attack, led by Major Potapov."

"I see," Potapov smiled. "And you will coordinate the assault, Comrade Colonel?"

"That's my job, Major," Burov confirmed. "Naturally, we'll get a reconnaissance report before any of us attacks the alleged enemy site."

"That can be best done from the air," Shalnev declared. "If a single helicopter flies over their position, the American hoodlums won't have any reason to be suspicious. The mountain they claim to be stationed at is not located within Glacier National Park, but it is close enough that they have probably seen Olsen's aircraft before."

"Assuming they've been at the mountain often enough to be familiar with Olsen's helicopter service," Potapov added. "Tell your reconnaissance pilot to be very careful."

"I will try to be careful, Major," Shalnev assured him.

"You're too valuable to risk on a recon mission, Major Shalnev," Burov told him. "Send someone else."

"If we are going to order men to risk their lives," the paratrooper replied, "then we should show them we are willing to take the same risks ourselves."

"Your men already regard you as a hero," Burov commented. "I'm certain you'll be awarded the Gold Star. Perhaps even the Marshal's Star. Not to mention a promotion to lieutenant colonel."

"I'm flying the recon mission, Colonel," Shalnev insisted. "I have to do this for my sake, as well as the sake of my men."

"What does that mean?" The KGB officer frowned.

"If you don't understand," Shalnev replied, "I can't explain the reason."

Major Shalnev took two paratroopers in one of the HH-1K choppers. The radio had been altered to a frequency matching the transceivers used by the ground forces.

As the helicopter approached the mountain range where the mysterious American commando unit was supposed to be waiting for the Russian strike force, Shalnev concentrated on piloting the aircraft while his men scanned the area with binoculars. The terrain was remote, miles from towns and villages. Shalnev frowned as he noticed a log cabin near the peak of a mountain.

"Scan the area carefully," the commander ordered. "We're approaching the enemy stronghold."

"Not much of a stronghold," one of the paratroopers commented, gazing through his field glasses. "I see many boulders and rocks below, but no one is moving."

"There does not seem to be enough natural camouflage to conceal a large number of men, Major," the other soldier stated. "Perhaps ten or twelve men, but I doubt if one could conceal more than that."

"I'm going to make a pass over the mountain," the major announced. "Watch for any movement from the cabin and the surrounding area."

The Bell whirlybird swung across the sky, flying directly over the cabin below. A paratrooper gasped when he spotted a long metal object braced on three metal stalks positioned in front of the cabin.

"There's a mounted machine gun below," the soldier announced. "And the barrel of a rifle jutting from one of the windows."

"Prepare to counterattack if the enemy starts shooting," Shalnev instructed.

"Da, Tovarisch," the second paratrooper replied, bracing himself behind a 7.62mm PKM machine gun mounted to the hull of the chopper.

"Hold your fire unless the enemy attacks," Shalnev ordered. "This is a recon mission, not an assault. The enemy probably won't shoot because they can't be certain we're not a harmless civilian aircraft. If we don't act in a hostile manner, they'll probably hold their fire, as well."

The major steered the chopper in a wide circle around the mountain. The Russians found little except rocks and boulders on the several levels and ridges. Only the east side of the mountain was exceptionally steep. The other sides of the mountain were more gradual slopes. Too rough for vehicles, but easy to climb. One would not need ropes and pitons except to scale the east wall. A rope extended from the base of a Rocky Mountain juniper on a cliff at the east wall, which suggested the enemy commandos planned to use it for an emergency exit.

"I think we've seen enough," Major Shalnev announced. "Let's head back to base and report to the colonel."

"Sir," one of the paratroopers began. "Do you think we'll attack the Americans tonight?"

"I believe the colonel will want to launch the attack as soon as we return," Shalnev replied.

21

Major Shalnev's prediction proved to be 100 percent accurate. When Colonel Burov heard the details about the mountain he was obviously delighted. The American gangsters might think they were prepared to repel an assault force coming up the mountain but Colonel Burov's tactics would be more thorough than that. He planned a three-pronged strike. Ground forces would attack from the south, north and west walls—as the Americans no doubt expected—but Russian paratroopers would also scale the east wall. And the three stolen helicopters would launch an attack from the air.

The Americans would probably expect them to attack at night, the KGB colonel reasoned. In fact, combat in the dark would probably be more advantageous to the Americans than it would be to Burov's troops. Thus, he ordered the attack to begin immediately. Russian soldiers climbed into trucks and choppers and headed for the mountain. Burov, however, ordered Captain Myshko to start the engine of an old Jeep they'd found at Olsen's.

"We'll have to find a position where we can observe the battle," Burov explained as he climbed into the Jeep beside his driver. "Close enough to see the outcome, but far enough away to allow us to observe the entire conflict."

"If we get too close we might fail to see the rest of the forest by looking at only a few trees, eh?" Myshko asked, glancing over a road map.

Naturally, this also meant they would not be in danger of being shot and they would be in an ideal position to make a hasty escape. Myshko realized this, but did not mention these things to Colonel Burov. The captain would be fortunate enough to avoid the battlefield because he was Burov's aide. Why tempt fate by implying Burov's reasons for observing the battle instead of participating in it might have more to do with personal survival than duty to the Soviet Union?

THE THREE BELL HH-1K helicopters rapidly flew toward the target area. Below, two tractor-trailer rigs full of Soviet troops sped along the road to the base of the mountain. Russians poured out of the vehicles and rapidly encircled the site as the choppers whirled overhead like birds of prey preparing to swoop down on their quarry.

The first chopper was piloted by Major Aleksei Shalnev. He approached the cabin and shifted the pressure to the cyclic as he pressed down on the collective. The helicopter swooped low as it passed over the roof of the wooden structure. Two paratroopers in the fuselage quickly yanked pins from F-1 fragmentation grenades and dropped the blasters on the target below. They immediately reached for two more red canisters, and as the chopper rose swiftly, the commandos tossed the second pair of grenades.

The F-1 frag bombs exploded, blasting huge chunks from two sides of the cabin. The next explosion was a double dose of thermite and the murderous liquid fire splashed across the remnants of the shattered building. Columns of black smoke rose from the wreckage as Shalnev's craft swung away from the site.

As a second chopper swooped into position, two PKM machine guns opened fire from the fuselage. Steel-jacketed 7.62mm bullets slashed into the burning rubble in case anything had managed to survive the first explosive attack. The third helicopter advanced quickly, ready to supply cover fire if needed.

Without warning, a fish-shaped projectile streaked across the sky like a deadly comet. It sailed into the second chopper before the whirlybird could complete its pass. The rocket exploded on impact and the copter burst into a sphere of fiery destruction. A split second later another rocket crashed into the third chopper. The brilliant explosions burned in the sky like supernovas as chunks of metal and mangled pieces of human bodies rained down on the charred remnants of the cabin.

"Holy Mother," Major Potapov gasped as he gazed up at the scene of the carnage through a pair of binoculars. "The enemy fired rocket launchers!"

"Ground Unit," Shalnev's voice spoke from Potapov's transceiver. "Enemy rockets fired from a cluster of boulders to the east. I can't see more than that."

"Too dangerous for you to stay airborne, Sky Unit," Potapov said into the mouthpiece of his radio. "Return to home base."

"Negative, Ground Unit," the paratrooper officer told him. "I'm going to land and join Ground Unit."

"I know better than to argue with you, Sky Unit," Potapov stated. "Be careful."

"You too, Ground Unit," Shalnev replied.

Potapov returned the radio to his belt and gathered up an AK-74 assault rifle. He turned to the men under his command. More than one hundred Russian soldiers, Potapov thought. His fellow countrymen whom he was about to order to charge into a battle with a clever and resourceful enemy. The GRU officer knew he would be ordering many of these men to their death. Potapov did not want that responsibility, but he realized if he failed to do so Colonel Burov would simply execute him for treason and send someone else to lead Russian troops into a bloody carnage that none of them wanted and none understood.

"Let's go," Potapov said grimly.

The Russians advanced up the west, north and south sides of the mountain. They carried an assortment of Soviet and American weapons, holding their fire, waiting for a target to present itself. Yakov Katzenelenbogen watched their progress from a crevasse near the peak. The Israeli grabbed a Galil rifle and placed the metal stock to his left shoulder.

Katz's Uzi hung from a shoulder strap and he also carried a SIG-Sauer pistol in shoulder leather and an Eagle .357 Magnum autoloader on his belt in a cross-draw position.

Calvin James, positioned beside Katz, had lowered the LAW rocket launcher and reached for his M-16 assault rifle. The black man wore his Jackass Leather shoulder rig with the Colt Commander under his left arm and the G-96 dagger under his right. James also carried a .357 Colt revolver on his hip. His M-16 was equipped with the M-203 grenade launcher and a Bushnell scope.

Hidden within a natural cave, which had been concealed with a dogwood shrub, David McCarter and Rafael Encizo grabbed their rifles. The Cuban had selected an H&K 33 assault rifle for the occasion while his British colleague was armed with a NATO L1A1, the English version of the famous Belgian FN FAL automatic rifle. Both men also carried their favorite pistols and machine pistols, as well as backup weapons, including another LAW rocket launcher.

Gary Manning, stationed by a cluster of boulders near the crevasse where Katz and James were positioned, had claimed first blood when he shot the choppers out of the sky. James had immediately blasted the backup copter. Manning, the expert marksman, was armed with an FN FAL with a Bushnell scope. He was also packing his Remington shotgun and an Israeli Eagle pistol in shoulder leather. Naturally the Phoenix Force demolitions pro carried his backpack of explosives, as well as a remote-control device to activate certain radio-operated contraptions that the Russian invaders would soon learn about—much to their dismay.

All five members of Phoenix Force aimed their rifles with care, peering through telescopic sights and taking care to shield their lenses from sunlight that could glitter on glass and betray their positions to the enemy. They waited for the Soviet troops to draw closer. The Russian paratroopers were well trained and moved from rock to rock, exposing little for the defenders to shoot at.

One Russian was a bit slow ducking behind a boulder. He only exposed the top of his head, but that was enough for Gary Manning. The Canadian squeezed the trigger when the cross hairs of the Bushnell found the fellow's forehead. A 7.62mm projectile smashed into the Russian's hairline, and the bullet sheared off the top of the commando's skull and burned through his brain, killing the soldier in the twinkling of an eyelash.

Other Russians rose and opened fire in the direction of the muzzle-flash of Manning's FAL rifle. Bullets sizzled and ricocheted around the Canadian warrior as he huddled to avoid the deadly hailstorm of full-auto slugs.

The other members of Phoenix Force did not allow Manning to draw enemy fire for long. Calvin James fired his M-16, pumping a 5.56mm round through the neck of a Russian paratrooper. The bullet splintered vertebrae and snapped the trooper's spinal cord. He tumbled lifeless down the mountainside while another Soviet soldier swung his AK-74 toward James's position.

Yakov Katzenelenbogen seldom used a rifle because it was a bit awkward for the one-armed Israeli. The long-barreled weapon was difficult to control using only his left hand and the trident hook device at the end of his right arm. This time, however, Katz used a boulder for a bench rest, which helped him control the Galil. He gazed through the scope and saw the cross hairs mark the center of a Russian soldier's chest.

Katz squeezed the trigger and a 5.56mm hornet struck the Soviet Trooper in the solar plexus. The Russian doubled up in agony and Katz fired a second round through the top of the wounded man's skull. The Soviet's corpse was kicked backward and rolled across the rocky surface toward the base of the mountain.

Encizo and McCarter joined in the firefight. A 7.62mm L1A1 missile bit into a Russian's chest, drilling through his heart. Encizo's H&K 33 sent a 5.56mm messenger into the side of another Soviet gunman's head. The copper-jacketed bullet knifed through the fellow's brain and blew out a chunk of skull when it exited just below the right temple.

"Are those damn machine guns in place?" Potapov shouted at his troops.

A voice belonging to one of the three men stationed behind an RPD light machine gun replied in the affirmative.

"Then fire, damn it!" the GRU officer commanded. "Spray them with enough bullets to cut off the top of their damn mountain!"

Three Soviet chatterguns erupted, firing hundreds of 7.62mm slugs at the Phoenix Force defenders. All five men were forced to duck under cover as swarms of high velocity bullets bounced against stone and sliced through air. Manning decided it was time to unleash the first remote-control surprise. He pressed a button.

Claymore mines, positioned on all sides of the mountain, were detonated by a low-frequency radio signal. The murderous blasts tore a dozen Russians to pieces. Shrapnel bombarded others. Soviet troops fell, dead or wounded. A cloud of dust rose from the mountain as bloodied human debris rained on survivors.

"Keep firing!" Potapov shouted. "We've got to advance or we'll never get the bastards. Charge!"

The major personally led the advance. He was not the sort of commander to stay back while others risked their lives. The Soviet invasion unit swarmed up the mountain like red driver ants. Manning watched them approach, his finger poised on another button of the remote-control panel.

"Now," the Canadian whispered, jamming his finger down hard.

A new radio signal activated the receivers of the robot units hooked up to three mounted machine guns. The weapons spat volleys of rapid-fire death, revolving on their mounts like the pendulum of a metronome in a macabre concert of destruction.

Russians shrieked as bullets lashed through their strike force. Major Potapov dropped flat, hugging the rock wall to stay below the salvos of high-velocity projectiles that burned the air all around him. Others were not as fortunate. Their bodies twiched and convulsed as blood spat from angry holes in their torsos, limbs and faces.

A few Russians bolted for cover behind boulders along the rock wall, throwing themselves into the matted shrubs that filled every convenient shelter. The branches fell apart under their weight and the men screamed as sharp wooden lances pierced their flesh. Three men were impaled on the treacherous stakes like bugs in a bizarre collector's box.

One man felt the shrubs give way and glimpsed the sharpened stakes in time to throw himself to the ground. He bellowed in agony as he felt other wooden points punch into his stomach and chest. Another Russian had landed sideways against a boulder, driving stakes through his right triceps and thigh muscle. The man cried out and recoiled from the shelter to lose his balance and roll painfully to the base of the mountain.

"Bloody hell," McCarter muttered, peering from his cover. "It worked."

Russian soldiers armed with AGS-17 grenade launchers opened fire on the machine gun nests, lobbing several 30mm explosive projectiles at the defenders' machine guns. Rock and metal burst into the sky as the grenades blasted the robot guns into scrap.

The roar echoed off the rock walls and for a few seconds the Soviets were uncertain if the machine guns had ceased fire. When they realized the shooting had stopped, a collective cheer rose from the Russian paratroopers.

"Don't claim victory too soon!" Major Potapov warned. "We must make certain all the American butchers are dead. Continue to advance with care."

The GRU officer tried to estimate how many men he had left. Potapov figured that more than half the Russian assault force had already been killed or severely wounded. What sort of demons were these American commandos, he wondered. Potapov prayed to any god who would listen to him to let the battle be over.

At the east rock wall a squad of fourteen commandos had moved into position. They had brought climbing gear to scale the steep surface, but the rope that hung from the cliff above offered to make their job easier. The Americans had obviously left the rope as an emergency exit, and any rope a man could climb down, another could climb up.

One of the Russian paratroopers grabbed the rope with both fists and pulled hard to test it. The yank tugged a large canvas bag from the base of the juniper trees on the cliff above. Several wires extended from holes in the sack, the lines securely nailed to the trunk of the tree. As the Russian's tug pulled the bag over the edge, the wires were drawn taut until they burst from the sack.

Each had a grenade pin attached at the end.

The canvas bag sailed down to land among the startled group of Russian soldiers. Most were puzzled by this unexpected delivery. As one reached down to see what was in the sack, two others realized it might be a trick. They bumped into each other as they fumbled for the bag.

"Nyet!" someone shouted.

Half a dozen M-26 fragmentation grenades exploded. The Russians were transformed into a flying collection of dismembered parts, including a single severed head. There was not enough of any man left to fit in a shoe box to be mailed back to the Soviet Union.

"Sounds like somebody found my rope," Calvin James whispered, noticing that the roar of the explosion came from the east wall.

The Russians who were advancing up the mountain also heard the blast. They turned toward the sound, and Phoenix Force took advantage of the distraction. The five-man army opened fire with their assault rifles on full-auto, and another wave of bullets lashed into the Soviet troops. More Russian corpses played "Jack and Jill" as they tumbled down the hill with more than a broken crown.

Two of the Soviet grenaders were among the bodies. The other two crouched behind their AGS-17 automatic launchers and fired at the Phoenix Force defenders. Two

30mm shells crashed into a cluster of boulders near Mc-Carter and Encizo and the pair ducked into a cave, but the grenades exploded close enough to their position to bounce them against the stone walls with the shock waves.

Calvin James moved his hand to the M-203 launcher attached to the barrel of his M-16. He aimed carefully and squeezed the trigger. The M-203 uttered a deep-throated bellow as it ejected a 40mm explosive projectile and the grenade hurled into the figurative lap of one of the Soviet soldiers. The high-explosive load blasted the Russian and his fancy AGS-17 gun into chunks of raw meat and scrap metal.

The last Russian with an automatic grenade launcher turned his weapon toward James's position, unaware that Gary Manning had switched his FAL rifle to semiauto for greater accuracy as he peered through the Bushnell scope. The cross hairs found the grenader's head, and Manning fired a 7.62mm round that smashed into the Russian's skull above the left ear. The bullet tunneled through the soldier's brain and burst a gory exit hole at his right temple.

"You shitty bastards!" David McCarter shouted as he emerged from the cave, blood trickling from a gash in his forehead.

The British ace was mad as hell about being knocked around inside the cave and he intended to let the Russians know he was pissed off. McCarter pulled the pin from an M-26 hand grenade and lobbed it at the advancing Soviets. The minibomb exploded, sending three Russians hurtling down the mountainside.

Rafael Encizo followed McCarter's example and hurled two more grenades at the Russians. Lobbing objects downhill was obviously easier than throwing them uphill, but a couple of Soviets tried. They yanked pins from F-1 frag grenades and tossed them at the Phoenix defenders. One fighter was careless enough to stand up to throw his grenade and Katz blasted him with the Galil before the soldier could make his throw. Instead, the Russian grenade rolled down the mountain to explode among Soviet troops near the base.

Another F-1 burst a chunk of rock and shrubbery several yards from the five-man army. Only one grenade landed near McCarter and Encizo. The Briton sneered at the pineapple as if it was a mere annoyance and kicked it over the ridge to send it hurtling back at the Russians. Two more Soviet troopers were blown to bits when the F-1 exploded.

The Russians were steadily driven toward the north wall. Manning nodded with grim approval and pressed another button on his deadly remote-control unit. A Claymore mine, positioned at the north summit, exploded and the blast hurled a dozen Russians down the mountainside, including Major Potapov. Shrapnel sliced into many more. The Soviet assault unit lay stunned, bloodied or dead, their bodies littered across the rock walls.

"That's it," Katz announced to the other members of Phoenix Force. "Let's mop up what's left."

22

Major Shalnev had landed his helicopter approximately a quarter of a mile from the mountain. He and three Russian paratroopers force marched to the battle zone as the conflict reached its frenzied zenith, approaching the east wall where the ghastly remains of fourteen grenade-ravaged Russian troops were scattered across the base of the mountain.

"Damn those butchers!" one of Shalnev's men rasped, clutching his stomach with revulsion.

"They did not use their climbing gear," Shalnev noticed. "The rope that extended from the cliff must have triggered a booby trap. Our opponents are not only clever, they are treacherous, as well."

"What should we do, Major?" a paratrooper inquired.

"Gather up the ropes and pitons," Shalnev instructed. "We will continue where our comrades began."

The four paratroopers skillfully scaled the steep rock surface, using hand and footholds where possible and hammering pitons into the stone for the ropes when needed. A grappling hook was hurled and it snared the trunk of the juniper tree on the cliff. The hook held fast and the Russians used the rope attached to the grappler to climb the mountain to the top.

Two paratroopers hauled themselves over the lip of the cliff, unslinging PPS submachine guns from their shoulders as they scanned the rock formations and boulders for a sign of the enemy.

"Drop your weapons and raise your hands!" Gary Manning's voice ordered as the Canadian warrior peered around the edge of a boulder, his Remington shotgun held ready.

Both Russians whirled toward the sound of Manning's voice and the Phoenix pro fired his l2-gauge blaster. A burst of double O buck slammed into one paratrooper's chest, the impact hurling the Russian over the edge of the cliff. He screamed briefly as he plunged to the ground below.

The other Russian triggered a 3-round burst from his PPS subgun, and bullets chipped the edge of the boulder Manning used for cover. The Canadian ducked low, pointed his Remington at the second soldier and fired off another load of l2-gauge devastation. The Russian's body was pitched sideways off the cliff, and began a silent descent to the ground below.

Manning cautiously approached the juniper tree, moving toward the rope that extended from the hook. Using the shotgun barrel, he poked the taut cord. Someone was climbing up the rope. Manning stepped to the lip of the cliff and aimed the Remington down at the figure scaling the wall, grabbing the rope hand over hand.

Suddenly powerful hands seized the barrel of Manning's Remington and a violent tug yanked the Canadian off-balance. He had to release the shotgun to prevent being hauled over the edge of the cliff, and he threw himself sideways into the juniper and clung to the branches to avoid plunging over the stone lip.

Major Shalnev had heard the shotgun blasts and clung to the rock wall, waiting for the enemy to check the rope. Manning had seen the last Russian paratrooper climbing up the rope, but he had not noticed Shalnev until the major ripped the shotgun from his grasp. The paratrooper commander discarded the shotgun and drew a Makarov from a hip holster.

Shalnev hauled himself over the lip of the cliff, pointing his Makarov at Manning. The Canadian stepped forward and lashed out a boot, kicking the pistol from Shalnev's hand. The Russian cursed as he fell and rolled on the ground. A PPS submachine gun was still strapped to his back, and as Shalnev started to unsling the weapon, Manning drew his .357 Eagle autoloader from shoulder leather.

"Don't try it, fella," the Canadian warned. "Use your left hand to grab the barrel and toss that gun over the side."

Shalnev looked at Manning, shrugging his shoulders slightly.

"You'd better understand real quick," Manning snapped, "or I'm going to blow your head off."

"Fuck you," Shalnev said in a dull monotone, but he unslung the PPS and hurled it over the cliff.

Suddenly the last paratrooper pulled himself up over the edge of the cliff. The Russian raised a Stechin machine pistol in his right fist, and Manning promptly shot him in the face, pumping a .357 slug betwen the man's eyes.

Major Shalnev took advantage of the distraction and lashed out a reverse roundhouse kick to Manning's forearm. The blow jarred the Magnum pistol from the Canadian's grasp, and Shalnev's left fist crashed into Manning's jaw while his right rammed into the Phoenix warrior's stomach. The Canadian gasped and tried to throw a punch at his opponent, but Shalnev's left hand struck like an ax against his collarbone. Manning fell to all fours.

Shalnev raised his hand to deliver a crippling karate chop to the seventh vertebra at the base of Manning's neck. Manning suddenly grabbed his opponent's ankles and yanked. Shalnev went down hard, his back slapping the rocky surface of the cliff.

Manning tried to twist Shalnev's legs and flip the Russian onto his belly, but the major did not oblige. He thrust his legs out, kicking Manning in the chest. The Canadian was sent sprwling as Shalnev jumped to his feet and assumed a karate stance, hands poised like twin hatchets ready to thrust and slash.

The Phoenix commando quickly rose as Shalnev charged, but the Russian turned sharply and shot a fast sidekick to Manning's belly. The Canadian groaned and folded at the middle from the powerful kick. Shalnev followed with a cross-body chop aimed at Manning's temple.

The Canadian's hands rose to snare his opponent's arm, and he twisted the Russian's limb and pivoted under it, pulling hard. Shalnev's body whirled into an abrupt somersault and crashed to the earth. But the tough Russian swiftly rolled back onto his shoulders and swung a boot high. The steel toe smashed into Manning's face, and the Phoenix warrior groaned as he staggered backward, blood trickling from his gashed cheek.

Shalnev scrambled to his feet and attacked, launching a hook kick with his left foot at Manning's ribs and a right-hand karate chop at the Canadian's neck. Manning blocked the kick with a hand stroke to Shalnev's shin and raised a forearm to stop the Russian's slashing hand.

Manning's fist smashed into Shalnev's jawbone, and he quicly clasped his hands together and swung a double-fisted chop to the Russian's breastbone. Shalnev moaned and began to stumble, but Manning quickly grabbed the major's head. He pivoted sharply and pulled hard, sending Shalnev tumbling head over heels to the ground.

The Russian rolled and sprang to his feet once more. He charged Manning, flashing his arms in a quick feint. Shalnev threw a high roundhouse kick at the Canadian's head, but Manning ignored the feint and raised his hands to snare the attacking legs. The Phoenix warrior turned swiftly and hauled his opponent in a rapid circle. Hopping on one foot, the major was easily thrown off-balance and hurled over the lip of the cliff.

Major Alekski Shalnev screamed as he plunged to the ground three hundred feet below, his body exploding on impact with the boulders at the base of the mountain. Manning staggered away from the cliff, struggling to catch his breath.

The battle was over. Dead Soviets dotted the mountainside. Only a handful of the Russian assault force survived. Most were wounded, unable to fight. Major Potapov lay sprawled beside a boulder, the back of his head cracked open, the rock splattered with his blood and brain tissue. None of the other officers had survived the carnage. Bewildered and without a leader, the remaining soldiers had no choice but to surrender. They simply had no idea what to do next. A few committed suicide, fearful of torture at the hands of their captors.

The men of Phoenix Force herded the Russians to the base of the mountain at gunpoint as Manning wearily shuffled down the rock wall to join his teammates. Katz noticed the bruises and bloodstains on the Canadian's face.

"Are you hurt, Gary?" the Israeli inquired.

"I'm okay," Manning assured him. "Looks like we won the last round. But my cover's burned. What'll we do about that?"

"Worry about it later," Katz replied. "The KGB failed in a pretty grand-scale mission and that means they won't come after us for quite a while. This has cost Moscow dearly and they won't want to repeat this mistake. So, for now, it's over."

"Yeah," Manning said. "For now."

COLONEL BUROV'S HANDS were trembling as he lowered a pair of binoculars. He could not believe what he had seen. Five men, just *five men*, had successfully wiped out the entire attack force. How was such a thing possible? What sort of human killing machines had the Americans recruited for this unique warrior team?

"Comrade Colonel?" Captain Myshko asked as he stood beside the KGB commander. "What shall we do now?"

"We've failed, Captain," Burov said grimly. "We cannot return to Moscow."

"But Colonel..." Myshko began.

"There is only one thing left to do," Burov declared, drawing his Makarov pistol from its holster.

"I see, Colonel," Myshko said, his voice trembling.

"Do you, Comrade?" the colonel inquired.

He suddenly jammed the muzzle of his Makarov under Captain Myshko's jaw and squeezed the trigger. The 9mm slug blasted through the roof of Myshko's mouth and plowed into his brain, killing the junior officer instantly. Burov took a handkerchief from his pocket and wiped his fingerprints off the Makarov and tossed the pistol in some bushes.

"Sorry, Captain," he told the corpse as he knelt beside Myshko's lifeless form to take the car keys from the dead man's pocket. "But I can't afford to have you contradict any details of the story I intend to tell the American authorities when I tell them I wish to defect."

Colonel Burov climbed into the Jeep and started the engine. Great Falls was the largest city in the area. If he hurried, he could be there before nightfall.

You don't know what NONSTOP HIGH-VOLTAGE ACTION is until you've read your 4 FREE GOLD EAGLE NOVELS

LIMITED-TIME OFFER

Mail to **Gold Eagle Reader Service**

In the U.S.
2504 West Southern Ave.
Tempe, AZ 85282

In Canada
P.O. Box 2800, Station A
5170 Yonge St.,
Willowdale, Ont. M2N 6J3

YEAH! Rush me 4 free Gold Eagle novels and my free mystery bonus. Then send me 6 brand-new novels every other month as they come off the presses. Bill me at the low price of $2.25 each—a 10% saving off the retail price. There are no shipping, handling or other hidden costs. There is no minimum number of books I must buy. I can always return a shipment and cancel at any time. Even if I never buy another book from Gold Eagle, the 4 free novels and the mystery bonus are mine to keep forever.

Name _____ (PLEASE PRINT)

Address _____ Apt. No. _____

City _____ State/Prov. _____ Zip/Postal Code _____

Signature (If under 18, parent or guardian must sign)

This offer is limited to one order per household and not valid to present subscribers. Price is subject to change.   166-BPM-BPGE

MYSTERY BONUS GIFT

HV-SUB-1